CW01003720

Author's Note

The outline for *Second Best* came into being during a visit to Minorca, a small island set like a jewel in the Mediterranean.

The core of any story lies in conflict of some form, and I have always believed that the sharpest conflict can be found within one person torn between desire and duty. In *Second Best,* Lisa is summoned to Minorca to attend her beautiful and headstrong sister Rachel's wedding to fashion photographer Carl Valdez. When Rachel postpones her imminent wedding and rushes off to a modelling assignment, Lisa is thrown into close contact with her future brother-in-law. As the magic of the island weaves its spell, she realises that she is falling in love and must choose between her growing attraction for Carl and her duty to her sister.

Another problem facing Lisa is that love is one of the strongest, most powerful, emotions known to the human race. When Rachel returns and a new wedding date is arranged, Lisa must either challenge the older sister who has always dominated her, or be witness to a marriage that will leave her alone with a broken heart.

Since Carl seems to look on her only as his fiancée's 'little sister', it appears that Lisa has no choice but to wish him and Rachel happiness in their marriage.

© Evelyn Hood July 1999

SECOND BEST

Evelyn Hood

This title, complete with new material by the author,
first published in Great Britain 1999 by
SEVERN HOUSE PUBLISHERS LTD of
9–15 High Street, Sutton, Surrey SM1 1DF.
Originally published 1984 by Mills & Boon under the title
Talk To Me Of Love and pseudonym of *Elizabeth A. Webster.*
This title first published in the U.S.A. 2000 by
SEVERN HOUSE PUBLISHERS INC of
595 Madison Avenue, New York, N.Y. 10022.

British Library Cataloguing in Publication Data
Hood, Evelyn. 1936-
    Second best
    1.   Love stories
    I.   Title
    823.9'14 [F]

ISBN 0-7278-5482-8

Printed and bound in Great Britain by
MPG Books Ltd, Bodmin, Cornwall.

CHAPTER ONE

THE door opened almost before Lisa had time to tug at the colourful bell-rope on the white wall.

'Mouse—darling!' her sister pulled her into a dim, cool room. 'Thank goodness you've arrived—I thought we were going to miss each other. What happened? Why did you take so long to get from the airport? Oh, I'll see to that—' She flipped open the handbag lying on the table, took money from it, and handed the sheaf of notes to the taxi-driver with a flourish. He put Lisa's cases down, took the money, and grinned at them both before going back down the stairs that led from the patio.

Lisa sank on to a soft, cushioned divan, blinking as her eyes tried to get accustomed to the shady room. She had been dazzled by the sun on her taxi-ride across Minorca.

'Rachel, you were supposed to meet me at the airport. I waited for ages, then I decided that I'd better come by taxi. I thought there must be something wrong.'

'Didn't anyone give you a message? Honestly, they're impossible!' Rachel said impatiently. She moved to the long mirror on one wall, pushing slim fingers through her red hair. 'Well, we haven't got time to talk now, my taxi's due at any minute. You'll manage to settle in by yourself, won't you, darling?'

'Settle in? Rachel, what are you talking about?' Lisa was completely bewildered. 'What taxi?'

'The taxi that's taking me to the airport, of course,' Rachel spoke as though Lisa should know everything without being told.

'But—Rachel, I'm here to attend your wedding, remember? You're getting married in two days' time!'

'But this marvellous assignment came up,' Rachel's eyes were bright as she turned away from the mirror. 'Mouse—a top magazine doing a huge fashion job in Paris. Just the breakthrough I've been waiting for! So I have to get over there—I haven't packed half the things I'll need——'

'But your wedding!' Lisa repeated helplessly. Rachel picked up a long green scarf from the table and knotted it quickly, carelessly around her throat. It added the perfect final touch to her tailored grey linen trouser suit.

'Mouse, for heaven's sake! Don't you understand? I can get married any time—I can't cancel a big modelling assignment for a wedding!'

'But——'

A horn beeped below the balcony.

'The taxi! Mouse, be a love and get the man to come up for the cases!'

Lisa obediently went on to the small, sunsplashed patio. The taxi was parked on the narrow dusty road before the apartment building. The driver, standing beside it, shaded his eyes as he looked up at the flower-bedecked balconies. When Lisa waved he nodded and disappeared into the arched entrance that led to the open staircase.

'What does your fiancé have to say about this?' Lisa demanded when she was back in the lounge.

Rachel zipped her travel bag shut briskly and slung it over her shoulder. 'Carl? He'll understand. After all, Mouse, he's a fashion photographer. He knows how these things turn up.'

'You mean he doesn't know yet?'

'I only heard this morning, and as he's in Madrid I could hardly talk things over with him, could I? But I sent a message. Just those cases,' Rachel said imperiously as the driver appeared. He swept a cool, appreciative glance over Rachel before bending to pick up the cases. Men's eyes always lit up when they saw Rachel. As he disappeared down the stairs, whistling, Rachel hugged Lisa, enveloping her in a cloud of the sophisticated scent that was almost her trademark.

'Take care—and have a lovely time. The rent's paid in advance, and the flat's yours. I'll get back as soon as I can.' And she went skimming down the stairs, the green scarf floating behind her.

'Rachel!' Lisa followed her down the first few steps. 'What if Carl turns up here? What am I going to say to him?'

Her sister stopped in the bend of the stairs, her magnificent tawny hair glowing like an exotic flower against the snow-white walls. Her face was small, neat, with wide, long-lashed green eyes and flawless skin. Rachel's beauty made her stand out in any crowd.

'Tell him I'll be back as soon as I can. And be nice to him, he's a pet.' She blew a kiss, then turned and sped on down the stairs. Lisa ran back to the patio and watched her sister being handed into the taxi as though she was very precious and fragile. Then the driver loped round to his own door, the engine started up, and Rachel's hand fluttered at the window as she was carried off. Lisa was, suddenly and a bit frighteningly, alone in Minorca.

The sun blinded her with its intensity. Inside, the flat was cool and shady. Unable to sit still, unable to get her thoughts into any order, she wandered from room to room. The lounge, cream-walled with red tiles on the floor, held two long cushioned divans and a beautiful refectory table with six rush-bottomed ladderbacked chairs. The kitchen was small, a sunny yellow room with dark grey tiles underfoot and wall cupboards with louvred doors to match the shutters on all the windows. There was a pale grey tiled bathroom in aquamarine with bath and shower, and two bedrooms. The main bedroom, with double bed and a huge built-in wardrobe, was fragrant with Rachel's perfume. A glass door led from the room on to a small balcony that overlooked gardens, with the sea in the distance.

Lisa carried her cases into the bedroom and began to unpack. The first dress she lifted out was a blue silky shift she had bought for Rachel's wedding. It had a neat mandarin collar and long full sleeves caught at the wrists. Trying it on in the shop, she had been pleased by the way the colour complemented her chestnut brown hair, hazel eyes and fair complexion. Now, in Minorca with its hot sun and its brilliant flowers, the dress looked dull and ordinary.

'Just like me,' she said aloud, opening the wardrobe. Although Rachel had taken two large suitcases with her, half the wardrobe was crammed with clothes—lacy, silky, fragile wisps in all the colours of the rainbow. Beside them the blue dress looked like a drab uniform. The contrast between her clothes and Rachel's depressed Lisa, and she shut the louvred doors firmly and went into the kitchen. She was hot and tired after the flight from England, she was upset by the bombshell her sister had thrown at her as soon as she arrived. Unpacking could wait until later.

'That is—' she told the refrigerator grimly, 'if I decide to stay. I can rush off at a moment's notice too, you know!'

The fridge was filled with food as well as a large jug of orange juice. Lisa reached out for it, then remembered the bathroom with its shower unit. She burrowed in a case for her dressing-gown, dropped her clothes casually, luxuriously, on the bathroom floor, pinned her hair on top of her head, and turned the shower on. The tepid water danced on her skin, setting up a glow from toes to shoulders. There was a large cake of flower-scented soap in the rack, and by the time she had towelled herself with one of the huge fluffy white and aquamarine towels and slipped her dressing-gown on she was feeling better.

She poured out a long cool drink, added ice, and carried it on to the patio, where she curled up in a large wicker chair, bare feet tucked beneath her. A pile of magazines lay on the small table. The top magazine was German, and Rachel's vivid, lovely face laughed from a nest of white fur on the cover. Her eyes were like emeralds, and one rounded bare shoulder could be seen rising from the fur.

Resentment welled up in Lisa as she stared at her sister's pictured face. She should have known better than to drop everything and come dashing to Minorca to please Rachel. She should have known that it would go wrong.

'You must be at my wedding, Mouse—you're all the family I've got now,' Rachel had coaxed during her long-distance phone call from Rome. 'I wouldn't want to be married without you beside me!' And Lisa had arranged a two-week break from the office, booked the flight, bought a dress, and packed in a whirl of excitement. It had all seemed so romantic. Everything connected with Rachel was romantic, and so different from the routine life that Lisa herself led.

'You're the clever one,' her father had told her when she was younger. She wasn't particularly clever. Secretarial college, a good job, friends, a steady boy-friend—hardly jet-setting. But she enjoyed her life. And there were the magic moments when Rachel whirled in from far-flung corners of the world, splitting Lisa's routine apart and bringing a breath of excitement and glamour with her.

Now Rachel had gone rushing off after more glamour, and this time Lisa had been dropped as abruptly as a stray leaf when the wind vanished. She sighed and went to the kitchen to refill her glass.

A car screeched to a halt outside. A door banged, then someone came running up the steps and Lisa heard the lovely wrought-iron gate leading to the patio being thrown back on its hinges. The door leading from the patio to the lounge burst open and a deep voice shouted angrily, 'Rachel? Rachel, where the hell are you? If this is your idea of a joke, I'll——'

He stopped abruptly as Lisa appeared at the kitchen door, then asked tightly 'Who are you?'

The sheer hostility in his eyes struck her dumb for a moment. She could only stand there, one hand clutching the door-frame, and stare at him. He was tall and lean, with a brown face dominated by those black hostile eyes fixed on her. His black hair was wavy and thick and almost too long, though it suited him. It grew down to brush the collar of a grey and white striped sweater.

'Well?' he demanded impatiently. He spoke English easily, but with a slight accent that showed that it wasn't his mother tongue. 'Who are you, I said—and where's Rachel?'

'She's not here. She's——'

'I don't believe you!' he cut across the words. 'She's hiding from me. Rachel!' he roared. Then he stormed into the main bedroom.

'Just a minute!' Lisa recovered from her

surprise and got to the door in time to see him snatch a dress from the open case on the bed. He dangled the material between his fingers, then tossed it down. 'This isn't Rachel's!' he said accusingly.

She pushed past him and slammed the lid of the case shut. 'No, it's not Rachel's, it's mine. And so is this apartment—so why don't you get out of it right now?'

'Where—is—Rachel?' he grated between his teeth. He caught her shoulders, shook her. Lisa felt as helpless as a kitten in his grasp. She pushed against his chest, which was as hard and unyielding as a rock.

'Let me go, or I'll scream the place down!'

He released her so suddenly that she almost lost her balance. They glared at each other, both breathless with rage. Lisa rubbed her arms, aware of pain where his fingers had bitten into her flesh. 'Rachel has gone to Paris,' she said, keeping her voice as level as she could. Obviously this man must be humoured and eased out of the flat as soon as possible.

His eyes were stormy. 'She can't have gone already!' he snapped, and turned away. She followed as he threw open the door of the spare bedroom, moved on to the bathroom, his deep voice roaring out Rachel's name.

'I told you—she's gone.'

'When did she go?' he asked suspiciously, moving back into the lounge.

'A few hours ago. Just after I arrived.'

'You?' He turned to survey her as though he

had only just realised that she was there. The dark eyes raked her from head to toe and she was suddenly aware that she wore only her old green dressing-gown, and that her hair, pinned up untidily, was escaping in tendrils to hang around her face.

'Ah yes, the little sister,' he said without interest.

'Since you seem to know who I am, perhaps you would tell me who you are, and what right you have to burst into my sister's flat uninvited?'

He blinked down at her, then his eyebrows rose. 'I have every right to—to burst in here, as you put it. I am Carlos Felipe Valdez. I am the man your sister promised to marry in two days' time,' he added accusingly, as though Lisa was responsible for Rachel's misdeeds.

'You're Carl?' She had expected someone much more mature, sophisticated. Not this hot-tempered man who stood over her, filling the placid apartment with suppressed power and fury. He was like a coiled spring. 'But you're supposed to be in Madrid!'

'I know—on urgent business. But when I received your sister's message I hired a plane and came back here to find out what she was playing at. When did you know of this?—this supposed visit to Paris?' His voice was still hostile, his eyes suspicious.

'When I arrived this afternoon.' Lisa hesitated, realising that he must be as taken aback at Rachel's flight to Paris as she was. 'Look, perhaps we should sit down and talk this over. Would you like some coffee?'

'You're lying!' he said abruptly.

'I'm what?'

'Lying. You knew that she had decided not to go through with the wedding. Nobody rushes off to Paris at a moment's notice!'

'Obviously you don't know——'

'A telephone message—that's all she sends!' He pulled a crumpled piece of paper from the pocket of his cream-coloured trousers and waved it at her. 'A telephone message, handed to me in the middle of a meeting! And she leaves you here to sweeten the blow, so that——'

Rage bubbled up in Lisa. This was too much! She had had a difficult day, she had been abandoned by her sister on an island where she knew nobody and couldn't speak the language, and now she was being accused of aiding and abetting Rachel! Her hands clenched at her sides and she moved forward aggressively.

'Now just wait a minute! I don't lie to anyone—not for my sister, and not about my sister. I came here, at Rachel's invitation, to attend her wedding. I arrived to be told that she was going off to work in Paris—and now I'm expected to put up with you and your ridiculous accusations! All I can say is that if you don't know my sister and her whims by now, perhaps it's as well that you're not going to marry her in two days' time!'

'Her—whims?' he asked, taken aback. The anger ebbed from his eyes, to be replaced by bewilderment.

'Her—her moods. If Rachel would rather work

in Paris than stay here and marry you, it's her decision. It's none of my business. And I most certainly wasn't left here to sweeten the blow. I can't think of anything I'd hate more. In fact, I'd appreciate it if you would just get out—now!'

She pushed past him and opened the door. He stayed where he was, toying with the crumpled paper in his hand.

'You asked me to stay for coffee,' he reminded her.

'I've changed my mind. Now I want you to go. You have no right to be in this apartment.'

He laughed, a short sound that still held angry undertones. 'Actually, I have. It's my apartment.'

Lisa felt as though someone had just thrown a bucket of cold water over her. 'Yours?'

'Mine.' His lips twisted as he read the expression on her face. 'You're jumping to conclusions, little sister.' Now that he was speaking normally instead of shouting the accent, though still faint, was more noticeable. 'I own this building. Rachel insist on paying rent. She isn't a kept woman—yet.'

Lisa lifted her chin defiantly. 'Rachel didn't explain that to me. I'll find a hotel——'

He reached her with one easy step and caught her arm as she began to turn towards the bedroom. As she looked up at the dark eyes directly above hers she felt the knot of hair loosen and tumble down to frame her flushed face.

'Don't worry—the rent's paid, you're entitled to stay here. I'll go. But if you happen to hear from Rachel tell her that I won't accept this—

what do you call it? A Dear John message? No, I don't accept that from anyone, not even Rachel!'

He crushed the paper in one hand and dropped it to the floor. His eyes travelled slowly, thoughtfully, over Lisa's face, her hair, her throat, then moved down and lingered. Following his gaze she realised that the dressing-gown had been pulled open, revealing rounded breasts beneath the thin material. She gasped, stepped back, and pulled the gown shut, holding the material tightly.

Carl Valdez laughed again, a sound with no amusement in it.

'Tell her, too, that if she did have ideas about you making it up to me she was wrong. You're not my type, little sister,' he said deliberately, and walked out, closing the door gently behind him. He managed to put more controlled force into the shutting of the door than he had used when he first threw it open.

Lisa stayed where she was, holding the neck of the dressing-gown about her throat, until she heard the car door shut and knew that he had gone. Then she went on to the patio and looked over the flower-laden wall as the engine roared into life.

The car, low and scarlet and open, took off with a cloud of white dust eddying from its tyres. Carl Valdez' black hair lifted and blew in the breeze as he went. He didn't glance up at the balcony where she stood watching until he was out of sight.

The engine's noise dwindled into silence, the white dust settled on the roadway again. For the second time that day, Lisa was left alone.

CHAPTER TWO

A plump, smiling woman in a black dress came up the stairs the next morning when Lisa was finishing breakfast on the patio.

'Dorita.' She tapped her rounded bosom with a stubby hand. 'You are the little sister, *si*? The little Mouse?'

'I'm Lisa Maxwell.' Lisa hated the pet name Rachel had given her when she was a baby.

'Lee-sah. It is pretty,' Maria nodded. 'Me, I look after the apartment every week. I see that there is food in the kitchen.'

She was like a breath of fresh air, with her twinkling dark eyes and her dimpled smile. She helped Lisa to unpack, chattering all the time in broken English.

'Beautiful, *no*?' she asked, touching Rachel's clothes with the back of her hand when she was hanging something in the wardrobe. 'She has lovely clothes, Señorita Rachel. And so many!'

'Did you know she was going to Paris?' asked Lisa.

'I was here, yesterday, when she was packing. Oh, she was so pleased to go!'

'Carl wasn't pleased when he came to look for her later.'

'Carlos is back?' Dorita shrugged. 'Well, he should have seen for himself that the Señorita is like a butterfly—always places to go, the need to be free. One man cannot catch a butterfly, not even a man like Carlos. Now, go and meet Minorca, Señorita Lisa, and I will clean the apartment for you.'

It was more of an order than a suggestion, and the sun was beckoning. Lisa put on a creamy cotton shirtwaister with flared skirt and three-quarter-length sleeves to protect her skin from the heat on this first day. She found a wide-brimmed straw hat in the wardrobe, with scarlet ribbons that matched the flowers patterning the hem of her skirt.

The apartments, a block of flats with flowers clustered thickly round each patio wall, were five minutes' walk from a fishing village. The country road gave way almost at once to a narrow street with houses and shops jostling each other. Lisa dawdled along, stopping to examine the goods on sale, or to listen to the whistling occupants of bird-cages hanging from almost every small balcony.

The street opened into a large harbour, the clear blue water enclosed within stone arms. One wall was broad and flat, close to the water's surface. Lisa strolled to the end, passing fishing boats that lay motionless by the wall. Fish clustered thickly beneath each keel, making the most of the shade the boats offered, and seeking shelter from the men and boys who were fishing off the end of the harbour.

The open water was like bottle-green glass, with the sun dancing like golden coins on the stony bed. When Lisa finally dragged her gaze away and turned, the entire harbour was spread before her, the brightly-painted boats and green splendour of sturdy palm trees contrasting with the stark white of the buildings. Beyond, the hills were shaded in greens, browns and golds, and above it all soared the blue sky, with only a white wisp of cloud here and there. To one side of the wide wall she had walked along was a sandy area massed with boats. Some were being built, some were being repaired, others lay beached on the yellow sand, piled high with nets, ropes and boxes. She went back along the wall, then stepped down on to the sand and wandered round the boats.

The hot warm air was heavy with the smell of fish, paint, and creosote. A long, sturdy shed carried a notice on its wall, advertising skin-diving, fishing trips, and boat trips round the island. Lisa thought, idly, that a boat trip on that cool, bottle-green water would be a good idea, but when she peered into the gloomy, jumbled depths of the shed, there was nobody there to give her information.

Someone was whistling cheerfully from beyond the shed. Lisa walked round the building and came on a large fishing boat on wooden supports. A man was busy painting it, his back towards her. He was dressed in faded blue jeans, ragged at the belt and torn off just below the knees to expose strong, muscled legs and bare feet. A smooth brown back rose from slim waist to broad shoulders, and as he worked, bending rhythmically to dip a paintbrush in a large tin at his feet, then swinging upright to slap crimson paint on to the wooden hull at eye level, the muscles rippled easily beneath his skin. Black curly hair shone in the sunlight as he worked.

He stopped whistling and swung round with a smile as Lisa passed—a smile that froze as their eyes met.

'Well?' said Carl coldly. 'Now what do you want?' He dropped the brush into the tin, glared down at her from his full height. 'If it's about your sister, I'm not interested—understand?'

She stared, as taken aback as he was.

'I didn't know—I was just——' she stammered over the words, aware that colour was flaming into her face.

'You mean it's just a coincidence, little sister?'

'My name is Lisa Max——'

'I know your name!' His voice was like a razor-sharp knife. 'Okay, so Rachel's been in touch with you, is that it? What do you both want? You want to be able to tell her I'm missing her—I'm heartbroken? Forget it—there are plenty more fish in the sea, tell her!'

'I wish you'd get it into your head that I have nothing to do with Rachel! I didn't know about Paris any more than you did!'

His cold expression didn't change. 'And stop bothering me!' He almost spat the words at her. 'I told you last night—you're not my type!'

'You really are the most pigheaded, bad-tempered man I've ever met!' she stormed. 'No wonder my sister isn't——' Then she stopped, horrified. Carl's guard had slipped for an instant before he turned away to slam a clenched fist into the boat's wooden side. Only an instant, but long enough for her to see the pain in his eyes.

'Carl——' she reached out to touch him, but hesitated before her fingertips touched the broad, tensed back. She hadn't stopped to wonder, until then, how he felt about things. He loved Rachel, and she had walked out on him. It was much harder for him to accept Rachel's disappearance than it had been for Lisa, but she hadn't done anything but shout back at him. And yet—looking at the set of his shoulders, the proud lift of his dark head, she sensed that pity was the last thing he wanted. She let her hand fall back to her side and waited until Carl's shoulders relaxed and he swung back to face her, his mouth twisted into a slight smile, his eyes carefully expressionless.

'You're probably right,' he said evenly. 'No wonder your sister isn't going to marry me.'

'I didn't mean it to sound like that. I'm sorry.'

He shrugged. 'Are you staying on in Minorca?'

'I'm on holiday for two weeks. I thought I'd wait for Rachel to come back.'

'I doubt if she will. But the flat's hers until the end of the month. There's nothing to stop you using it.'

'Except you.' As a question flared into the dark eyes, she added, 'I don't think you want me to stay in Minorca.'

He had gained control of himself again. He

looked her over slowly, casually, the same look that had burned into her on the previous evening. 'It means nothing to me. I just ask that you keep out of my way—and I'll keep out of yours.'

Obviously sympathy was wasted on this man, Lisa realised, humiliation and anger fighting within her.

'There's nothing I'd like better,' she said icily, and turned to go. As she moved, her foot hit against the large tin of red paint. The tin, half buried in sand, stayed where it was, but Lisa stumbled, swayed, reached out for support, and felt herself falling, seemingly in slow motion, against the sticky, freshly painted boat. Then a hand captured her outstretched fingers, a strong arm caught her about the waist, and she was pulled back firmly against Carl's body. She could feel the taut strength of him against her back, feel the warmth of his sun-kissed skin through the thin material of her dress. She twisted round in his embrace and Rachel's wide-brimmed hat fell to the ground.

Carl drew her outflung hand, still imprisoned in his, back from the wet paint, and she felt the tips of her fingers brush against his chest. His grip round her waist shifted slightly, pulling her closer. His eyes, when she forced herself to look up at him, were very close to hers. Suddenly she started to tremble. She knew that she should pull herself free of him, but she had no will of her own.

Carl's lips parted. His eyes moved over her face as though he was memorising every feature. Then, abruptly, he released her.

'And stay away from my boat. You almost ruined the paintwork.' He stooped with that easy, athletic movement she had seen earlier, and picked up the straw hat.

'Goodbye, Señorita Maxwell,' his deep voice said with crushing finality as she took the hat from his fingers. Then he turned away, picked up the brush, and went back to his work.

It was as though he had wiped her from his sight, from his mind, from life itself. Straight-backed, still trembling, Lisa walked as quickly as she could through the soft sand to the harbour wall.

Tears stung at the backs of her eyes, and her mind began to fill with the sort of remarks she should have made, but hadn't thought of. The colourful boats had lost their charm, she realised as she gained the stone wall and made her way back to the street fronting the harbour. The crystal clear water only revealed tins and bottles that had taken up residence on the sea-bed, and the sun stared down at her with a fiery, contemptuous eye.

She went into one of the open-fronted restaurants by the harbour, and ordered a fruit drink. When it arrived, in a tall cold glass musical with ice-cubes, she sipped the liquid slowly and concentrated hard on regaining her first enchant-ment on seeing the harbour.

Lisa rarely lost her temper, but at that moment she was raging inwardly at Rachel for putting her into such an impossible situation, and for Carl for taking his own anger out on her. She remembered, fleetingly, the spasm of pain in his eyes, then reminded herself that his misery was not her problem. He had no right to punish her for her sister's faults. No doubt Rachel was having a marvellous, exciting time in Paris, all thoughts of Minorca and Lisa gone out of her head. Rachel had an enviable ability to concentrate completely on the present, and even when she was a little girl she had preferred to close her mind firmly on guilty or unpleasant thoughts.

Lisa concentrated on the calm water before her, the motionless boats, the sweet, cool tang of her drink, and began to feel happier. She was on holiday, on a beautiful island. It was time she began to behave like a holidaymaker and got some fun out of her trip. She would get a map of the island, find out what sort of tours were on offer. She would send postcards to her friends, acquire a suntan, explore, swim. Her spirits rose.

A motor-bike roared past the restaurant, swerved out of sight round the corner, and stopped. The rider, a tall thin youth wearing crumpled shorts and sandals, ran down on to the beach, shouting and waving.

'Hey—Carlos!' His voice intruded on Lisa's thoughts, and she looked up. Carl could be seen from where she sat, she realised with some annoyance. He turned as the boy joined him and they both walked round the boat, inspecting it, hands moving rapidly as they talked. Then Carl put brush and paint pot into the shed Lisa had looked into earlier, shut the door, and followed the youth along the harbour wall. Lisa glimpsed his face as the two of them crossed the road and disappeared along the side of the restaurant. He was laughing, talking, his dark eyes brimming with amusement, his teeth gleaming white in a broad grin. One hand rested lightly on the boy's shoulder. He didn't notice Lisa, who sat just inside the restaurant, in the shade.

The motor-bike engine split the calm peace of the harbour, and was joined by a second engine. The youth's vehicle swung into sight round the corner, whipped past Lisa and sped on up the street. The second machine, with Carl astride the saddle, followed almost at once. She glimpsed his hands gripping the handlebars, his shoulders square and steady as he controlled the large, glossy machine, then he was past, roaring out of sight with the wind catching at his black hair.

Lisa finished her drink, taking plenty of time about it. Carl puzzled her, and despite her determination not to be involved in any way with her sister's love affair she found that her thoughts kept turning back to him.

She knew, from Rachel's sprawling, infrequent letters, that they had first met when Rachel was on holiday in Minorca. She had become involved in a photographic assignment while she was on the island, and Carl had taken the photographs. His name cropped up a few months later when he and Rachel worked together in Venice. And the letter from Venice had been followed almost immediately by an excited scrawl from Rome, announcing that Rachel and Carl were to be married.

'He insists on going back to Minorca for the wedding,' her handwriting had flamboyantly hurled itself across the notepaper, which carried the crest of a first-class hotel. 'So I'm here on a quick shopping spree first. I don't care where I marry him—just as long as I do! But you must be there, Mouse. If you aren't there as a witness, I might not believe it myself!!'

The letter had been chased by a telephone call, and Lisa had obediently hurried to Minorca— only to see Rachel tossing her wedding plans aside, as a spoiled child throws a toy away in order to reach for something new.

That was Rachel's trouble. Men just ran into her path; rich men, charming men, talented men—and always handsome men. How was she to know when she met Mr Right? Lisa sometimes wondered. Or had she met him already, and hurried on, leaving him on this island paradise?

She couldn't bring herself to believe that the tempestuous man in washed-out, ragged jeans was Rachel's Mr Right. Nor could she visualise him as a fashion photographer, used to the world of beautiful people that Rachel mixed with all the time. Why would a man like that paint boats and wear old clothes? Was the man she had met really Rachel's fiancé—or was he some sort of impostor?

She shook herself free of the fantasy she was beginning to entangle herself in. The only person who could tell her the truth was Rachel—and she would therefore have to wait until Rachel came back.

Whatever Carl was—and whoever he was—he was compelling, she realised with a slight smile as she walked back to the flat. He was certainly staying around in her mind, in spite of her determination to forget him. And he stuck there, drifting maddeningly in and out of her thoughts, for the rest of the day, as she swam and sunbathed at the pool near the flat.

The pool was just busy enough to be companionable, but not busy enough to be crowded. Most of the people there were from the holiday flats nearby, and as many of them were families staying in the vicinity of the paddling pool Lisa was able to swim without interruption, and to laze on a beach chair between dips in the cool, inviting water. Behind her, tall fronded grasses edged the sundeck, and steps led down to a cafeteria and bar.

From time to time groups of young men passed on their way to the pool, the bar, the tennis courts, or the cafeteria. Glancing up when their shadows fell across her, Lisa noticed admiration in most of the faces as they eyed her slim, rounded body in the yellow bikini. She guessed that if she was in need of company a smile would give sufficient encouragement for one or more of them to stop and talk. But she was beginning to enjoy being alone. The first panic was over, and in its place she was aware of a pleasant sensation of freedom.

Later, after a leisurely bath, she slipped into a crisp blue sleeveless dress with broad belt and full, pleated skirt. She was beginning to feel

hungry, and toyed with the idea of walking along
to one of the village's restaurants instead of
cooking something for herself. As she brushed
her hair until it shone she found herself wishing
that she was a more outgoing type, like Rachel.
By this time, Rachel would have made sure that
she had an amusing, charming companion for
dinner.

'You're looking for food, not romance!' she
lectured herself. 'You don't need a man!'

The wrought-iron gate rattled and someone
tapped lightly on the door. Lisa opened it, her
thoughts still on Rachel's ability to attract the
right escort for the right occasion—and stared at
the tall, good-looking man who leaned against the
door frame like a knight who had arrived to
rescue a damsel in distress.

CHAPTER THREE

'MIKE.' The visitor grinned down at Lisa.

She couldn't believe her eyes. It just wasn't possible to conjure handsome men out of mid-air by simply thinking about them. Or was it, on this flower-bedecked sunshine island?

'Mike Barclay?' This time there was a faint question in his voice.

'Mike——?'

'And you're Lisa. And Rachel forgot to tell you about me, right?'

'Right.' The reference to Rachel proved that he was real, not somebody she had dreamed up. 'I'm sorry, I didn't realise you were a friend of Rachel's.' She stepped back, opening the door wide, and he dipped his head to come through it, then dropped easily on to one of the divans.

'Rachel asked me to look after you while you were on the island. I should have guessed she'd forget to tell you about it.'

'She left in such a hurry,' Lisa explained.

'She did, didn't she?' he agreed. Lisa liked the look of him. He was broad-shouldered, with brown hair and grey laughing eyes. He had a dependable air about him.

'As I said, she asked me to look after you, so I thought we might start by having dinner tonight.

29

Sorry to spring it on you, but I've been busy with tourists all day—didn't have time to arrange things in advance. If you're booked we could make it tomorrow evening.'

'I'm not booked, but——' she hesitated, and his wide grin bathed her in its warmth again.

'You don't go out with strangers, is that it?'

'I thought you said you were a friend of Rachel's?'

'But how do you know that for sure?' he challenged. He was English, with a drawl that placed his home in the Bristol area, Lisa guessed. 'I might be a white slave trader—I hadn't thought about that until now.'

'You don't look like a white slave trader.'

'So——?'

'So where are we going to have dinner?' If the Fates saw fit to send a good-looking escort to her door just at the right time, why should she hesitate? Lisa thought, picking up her jacket and bag. Mike rose to his feet in one smooth movement and beamed down at her.

'Terrific! I know just the place, if you're in no hurry to eat. We'll go across the island to Alayor.'

The restaurant he chose was small and informal. Lisa's day in the open air had given her an appetite, and she enjoyed the meal he ordered for them both.

'Do you know Rachel well?' she asked as they finished eating.

He hesitated, then shrugged his shoulders. 'Does anyone get the chance to know Rachel well? We've been acquainted for a while.'

'You knew her before she came here to marry Carl?'

'I met her in England.' He signalled the waiter, and coffee was brought to the table. 'How do you like Minorca, Lisa?'

'I haven't had much time to get to know it, but I like what I've seen.'

'You'll love it,' he told her enthusiastically. 'I've been here for two years. I came for a holiday—and didn't want to go home. I'm co-owner in a boat business—fishing parties, skin-diving, and so on.'

Lisa recalled the inviting green water outside the harbour. 'Perhaps I'll book a boat-trip with you.'

'Any time,' he assured her, his grey eyes studying her with open approval across the table. 'Have you ever tried skin-diving?'

'I'd be afraid to.'

'You'd love it. I'll take you out tomorrow, I've got a free day——'

'But I'm not sure that I could handle it——' she began, but Mike swept her protests aside firmly.

'You never know until you've tried. By the time you go home you'll probably be an expert—and an enthusiast. Trust me. You're here for two weeks, aren't you?'

'That was the original idea, but I don't know if it's worth staying on now that Rachel's in Paris. But perhaps I should, in case she comes back soon.'

Some of the warmth ebbed from his face. 'Oh,

she'll be back. Rachel flits from place to place, hadn't you noticed? Like an empty-headed butterfly.'

His change of mood was unmistakable. 'You don't like her much, do you?'

'Not a lot,' he said evenly.

'I thought you said you were her friend!'

'No, you said I was her friend. I said we'd been acquainted for a while,' he reminded her. 'Rachel isn't the type to have friends. Admirers, yes. Lovers, yes. But friends—friendship means giving as well as taking, and Rachel never did have a lot of time for that sort of relationship. And there's no need to glare at me,' he added with lazy amusement. 'You don't have to feel that you must rush to your sister's defence. You're too adult to do that, surely?'

Lisa felt the colour flow into her face. 'If you feel that way about her, I don't know why you agreed to take me under your wing,' she said stiffly.

'Maybe I wanted to make a visitor to the island welcome. Maybe I wanted to find out what sort of sister Rachel would have,' he said maddeningly.

'And now that your curiosity's satisfied, perhaps you'd like to submit your report?'

'You're not like her at all. You're more human—when you aren't scowling at me like a protective sister.' He grinned, and in spite of her annoyance on Rachel's behalf, Lisa felt her lips twitch into an answering smile.

'Now that's much better,' Mike approved.

'What—what about the man Rachel's going to marry?' curiosity prompted her to ask. 'Do you know him as well?'

'Carl? Of course I know him. He's my partner.'

Lisa, about to take a sip of coffee, put the cup into its saucer, blinking across the table at Mike's cheerful face. 'Carl? But I thought he was a photographer?'

'One of the best, I'm told. But he's an islander first, last and foremost. He loves the sea. When I decided to stay here, he jumped at the chance of taking on a partner who'd be willing to mind the shop while he was away photographing beautiful women in expensive clothes.'

'And the apartment block? Do you own that as well?'

Mike shook his head. 'That's not my scene. Carl got the land as his share when his old man gave up the family farm. It couldn't be farmed, so he built flats on it. His father moved to Ibiza about ten years ago.'

'He doesn't look like a man with so many business interests,' Lisa said slowly. She recalled her last sight of Carl, bare-chested and in faded, ragged jeans, and found it hard to imagine him as a fashion photographer and property owner.

'He's got a good head on his shoulders. The man who's got it all, that's our Carlos.'

'Not quite all,' Lisa pointed out. 'He doesn't have Rachel.'

'Oh, I'm quite sure she'll come rushing back to his arms. After all, he's the ideal husband, for

Rachel. Looks good, knows the best people, plenty of money—just her type.'

Anger flared up in Lisa. 'Look, just because she isn't your idea of a wife it doesn't mean that she's——'

'You've met Carl, have you?' Mike drawled, as though she hadn't spoken at all. She gave him a brief description of the scene in the flat, and beside the boat, without going into detail about her feelings of humiliation.

'I can't imagine Rachel wanting to marry anyone as—as insufferable as that man!' she finished sharply.

'I told you—he's rich.'

She ignored the jibe. 'He looks so young. Somehow I'd thought of Rachel being interested in a more mature man.'

'He's in his early thirties, like me, and he can be very mature when he wants to be. He's even a nice guy, most of the time. But you've got to remember that he's got a lot on his mind just now. Rachel for one thing—it's no joke to find that your fiancée's walked out just before the wedding. And I happen to know that he hoped to get the marriage safely over before his family found out about it. They've lived here for generations, and Carl's the first one to consider marrying a foreigner. They could cause trouble.'

'Rachel didn't tell me.'

'I don't think Rachel knows. There's only his brother Eduardo left on this island, and Carl's made sure that he and Rachel never met. Eduardo's been on holiday, and I reckon Carl was planning to introduce him to Rachel when he got back—after the wedding, when it would be too late for Eduardo to object.'

'If he's so afraid of his family, I can't think why he's marrying Rachel at all,' Lisa said sarcastically.

'Carl's not afraid of anyone or anything. But he respects his family. I don't think he wants to be put into a position where he might have to go against them. On the other hand, if he and Rachel were already married, the family would have to accept it,' Mike pointed out, then added swiftly, 'Look—do we have to spend our first evening together talking about Rachel and Carl? Why don't we start concentrating on us?'

It was very easy to concentrate on Mike, Lisa found. He was fun to be with, and an excellent dancer. When they got back to the apartment it was very late, and he shook his head when she invited him in.

'Better get a good night's sleep. I'll pick you up in the morning, okay? Bring a swimsuit and I'll see to the rest of the gear.'

He waited till she had found her key and opened the door, then he took her into his arms and kissed her, his lips warm on hers. When he finally released her, his teeth gleamed in a grin.

'That's just a sample. I'm going to enjoy your holiday, Lisa. See you tomorrow.' Then he turned and loped swiftly, quietly, downstairs to his car.

Lisa refused to listen to the small panicky voice

that clamoured in her head next morning, when she woke to the realisation that she had committed herself to a diving trip. Telling herself firmly that she would be perfectly safe with Mike, and that she would probably have a wonderful time, she put on a new one-piece suit in narrow multi-coloured stripes, and studied herself before the full-length mirror.

The previous afternoon by the pool had flushed her body with the beginnings of a tan, and the suit shaped her neat hips, slim waist and rounded breasts attractively. She wasn't as lovely as Rachel, but she didn't look too bad, she knew. She put on a green shirt and white slacks, packed a beach bag, and was brushing her hair when she heard a car stop outside. With a thrill of excitement, she picked up her bag and hurried to the top of the stairs.

'I'm all ready——' The words faded as her visitor appeared at the bend of the stairs. The brown and gold striped shirt, open at the throat, and the brown slacks looked just right against the white wall. So did the dark eyes, the tanned face, and the mop of black hair. Lisa backed on to the patio.

'I'm just going out,' she said hurriedly as Carl reached the top of the stairs and stopped with one hand resting on the wrought-iron gate. 'Mike Barclay's going to take me skin-diving, so if you——'

'I know he is—or he was,' Carl's voice was polite, formal, his eyes carefully blank as they met hers. 'Mike has had to go to Mahon. One of the boats broke down, and it has to be repaired today.'

Disappointment welled up in her, to be pushed aside by sheer panic when his deep voice went on, 'He's asked me to take you instead.'

'No——' she said without thinking, then flushed as she realised how abrupt it sounded. 'I mean, I——'

Irritation flared in his eyes, sharpened his voice. 'I'm qualified, and experienced. And I'm a good diver.'

'I expect you are. But I don't want to take up your time. You must have better things to do.'

'As it happens, I've got a free day.'

'Then couldn't you have gone to Mahon?' she asked, before she had a chance to stop her own tongue.

Carl hooked his thumbs into his narrow belt. 'Mike's the expert when it comes to engines. Shall we go?'

He pushed the gate open, stepped aside, and waited. It was obvious that she wasn't going to be allowed to cancel the trip. Seething silently, furious with Mike for getting her into this impossible situation, she walked past him and began to descend the stairs.

A beach buggy waited outside. Carl took her bag, dropped it in the back, then scooped her up into the passenger seat as though she was a toy. They drove in silence to the harbour.

'Come on——' He lifted her from her seat and set off across the warm, gritty sand without looking to see if she was following. In the dim, crowded shed Lisa stood by while he selected equipment for the dive. His dark eyes flickered over her body with impersonal, businesslike interest, and he picked out an air-tank, harness, weighted belt and flippers.

'I think they'll do. Come here,' he ordered, and she went, meekly. He fitted the mask on, his fingers surprisingly gentle on her hair. 'Right, carry this lot.'

Loaded down with masks, flippers, and belts, she struggled behind him as he loped across the sand as though the tanks he carried weighed hardly anything. By the time she reached the buggy he was stowing everything away carefully.

'Get in.'

She would have liked to have refused, to feel free to walk away and leave him. But there was something in his manner, as he stood by the door waiting to help her into her seat, that warned her that he would not accept any signs of mutiny. He was quite likely to follow her if she marched away, toss her over his shoulder, and dump her in the back among the tanks and flippers, and she wasn't prepared to take that chance.

He seemed to forget that she was beside him as they drove inland, away from the sea. He was relaxed, handling the buggy with effortless grace, humming quietly under his breath as he watched the road unwinding before them. Lisa, too, concentrated on the roads, the brilliant gardens and small, neat red-earthed fields, each bounded by roughstone walls or wooden windbreakers. Now and then as the road twisted they met the sea again, a great palette of blues and greens merging to meet the sky on the horizon. Occasionally the calm water was dotted with yacht sails or the big multi-coloured sails belonging to wind-surfers.

The buggy turned off the main road and went along a smaller, dusty road for a mile before turning in at a wide gate set in high stone walls.

'Here we are,' Carl threw the words over his shoulder as he jumped down and came round to her side.

Lisa stared around as he lifted her down and began to fill her arms with diving gear again. They had stopped on a wide sweep of red gravel, edged with flowers and shrubs. Above her a white stone balustrade edged a large patio fronting a rounded house with huge sliding windows. From the gravel courtyard where she stood, paths and steps led off in every direction, disappearing into the colourful garden.

'This way.' Carl's voice prodded her out of her study of the great white house.

'Who lives here?' She had to hurry to catch up with him as he followed a path that led round the side of the house.

'I do, at the moment.'

'You?'

He looked back, laughed at the surprise that she knew showed in her face. 'Why not? I have to live somewhere. It belongs to my father.'

'But it's so——' Lisa stared up at the icing-white rounded walls soaring above them.

'So pretentious,' Carl finished the sentence for her. 'It was built for my mother, but now it's rented out to wealthy holidaymakers. For the moment, I'm using it.'

He led her up a flight of stairs at the rear of the house, and they emerged on to a broad terrace. A grey-haired woman watering plants in wooden tubs smiled at them, curiosity in her black eyes as they rested on Lisa. Carl spoke to her in swift, liquid Spanish, and she beamed at Lisa as she answered.

'This is Francisca. She looks after the house,' he told Lisa briefly. 'You've got your suit on?' His eyes travelled over the blouse and slacks she wore. When she nodded, he added, 'Better leave your clothes here.'

He unfastened his trousers, slipped them off, and began to unbutton his shirt. 'Good—no silly frilly suit that's going to get caught up in the harness.' There was a note of approval as he openly studied the streamlined suit she wore. She felt selfconscious—until she remembered that he was used to photographing women with better bodies than hers.

Carl loaded her yet again with diving equipment, then picked up the tanks and led the way down more steps, past a small blue-tiled swimming pool on a lower terrace, then down on to a path that ran between bright rock gardens into a belt of shady trees. Sunlight fell through the leaves above, dappling his lithe brown body, touching his thick black hair with gentle, caressing fingers.

A final flight of shallow steps brought them from the shelter of the trees to a secluded bay with low cliffs on both sides. Between their protective rocky arms the sandy beach sloped to calm green water that shaded to clear blue where the bay opened on to the sea.

Lisa stopped and stared, the sand hot beneath her bare feet. 'It's beautiful!' she exclaimed in awe. Carl shot her a quick smile, and she realised that she had said the right thing.

'Yes, it is.' He walked to the water's edge. A cluster of flat dark rocks lay to one side of the little bay, half in and half out of the water, and he put the tanks down beside them, then turned to take the rest of the gear from Lisa. 'I use it often for fashion work.'

'Does this belong to your father as well?'

He glanced round the bay, and at the white house on the cliff above. 'Yes. The house is built on an outcrop of rock, so it has this bay at the back, and another bay in front of it. He doesn't own the bay in front,' he added gravely, a gleam of amusement in his face as he turned back to her. 'He's not that rich.'

He began checking out the diving equipment.

'This is a different world from my two-roomed flat at home,' said Lisa. 'Do you realise how lucky you are to live on an island like this?'

Carl blew hard into a mouthpiece, put it down, and picked up an air regulator. 'Oh yes——' he said quietly, looking again at the bay then back at her, 'I know how lucky I am.'

In that moment before he went back to his

work, Lisa was allowed a glimpse the real man beneath the hot-tempered, caustic person she had first met in Rachel's flat. In that moment, she felt the first stirrings of attraction towards Carl Valdez.

CHAPTER FOUR

THE moment that held them together was gone almost as soon as Lisa recognised it.

'Come and sit on this rock while I get you fitted out——' Carl held out a hand, guided her to a flat rock. His voice was matter-of-fact again. 'The tank's heavy. You'll have to sit down until you get used to the weight of it, otherwise you'll lose your balance.'

His hands brushed lightly against her back, her shoulders, the swell of her breasts as he lifted the tank on to her back and helped to adjust the harness. His touch was completely impersonal and his face, close to hers as he checked straps and buckles, was expressionless, intent on his work. The nervousness that had fluttered through her at the first contact between his hands and her body vanished as the tank was settled into place and Carl buckled the weighted belt round her waist.

'Dip your feet in this pool and then put the flippers on as though they were ordinary shoes,' he instructed her, and held her steady while she obeyed. 'Now sit there—and don't try to get up.'

'I-I don't think I could!' Butterflies fluttered in her stomach, beneath the heavy belt, as she looked out at the sea and realised that she was about to venture beneath its sparkling surface.

43

Pulling on his flippers with practised ease and slipping a tank on to his muscled back as smoothly as though it was a jacket, Carl grinned down at her. He looked carefree, his teeth white and even against his tan, the smile illuminating a face she had begun to associate with chilly anger.

'Don't worry, I've never lost a pupil yet,' he said reassuringly. 'You'll enjoy yourself once we get into the water.'

It took quite a while to get her sense of balance once she stood up. She held tightly to Carl's hands, and concentrated on following his instructions. Then, slowly, they went into the shallows, walking backwards because of their flippers.

The water met her and shaped itself to her body like cool silk, soothing away the heat of the sun. The sandy bed was comfortable to walk on, and Lisa's first nervousness began to ease. When they were waist-deep Carl showed her how to defog her mask by rubbing the face plate with saliva and rinsing it in the sea. Then he helped her to put it on, and slipped the mouthpiece between her lips. To her surprise Lisa found that she could breathe naturally.

'So far so good. Now put your head beneath the surface. Go on!' he added, with an edge to his voice as she hesitated. 'Hold on to my hands. I won't let you go.'

Going under for the first time was difficult, but once she got used to the undeniable fact that she could breathe below the surface, she was so enchanted by the underwater world that fear was forgotten. Carl waited patiently until she had

gained confidence, then he took her as far as the
point where the bay opened out to the sea. He
stayed within reach all the time, guiding her, yet
letting her swim on her own, so that her
confidence increased. The water lifted his hair
into a halo about his head, and she felt her own
long brown hair drift behind her as she swam.
The surface was a bright ceiling and sunlight
danced in jewelled patches over the rocks and
sand below as they cruised through the warm
water. It was everything Mike had said it would
be. Lisa learned the joy of floating through liquid
space, turning and twisting like a leaf on the
breeze. Small fish gathered round her, bumping
gently against her body as she moved from an
interesting rock formation to a rainbow-hued
plant growth.

There was always something else to explore,
and she was disappointed when Carl touched her
arm and signalled that she had to follow him back
into shallow water.

The tank was heavy on her back as soon as she
stood up beside him, waist-deep in the sea. The
sun was warm on her shoulders. 'Let's go
back——'

'You've had long enough for a first time. Come
on—time to be a land animal again.' He took her
hand, led her in a clumsy, backwards walk to the
rocks, so unlike the free-moving, weightless
delight of underwater travel. When they reached
the rock she realised that she was tired, and
relieved to be free of the tank. She stretched her
arms as he took the tank off and laid it down.

'You're a good pupil.' He knelt to pull her flippers off.

'I love the sea,' she admitted. 'Rachel hates it.'

'I know.' The smile faded from his upturned face at Rachel's name, and Lisa could have kicked herself for her thoughtlessness. He got up, put the flippers neatly together and stowed them in a shady crevice between two rocks. 'Hungry?'

'I'm starving!'

'Well——' Carl moved to where the cliff rose from the sand and came back with a basket. He opened the lid, and Lisa stared at the food neatly arranged inside, together with a bottle of wine and glasses.

'Where on earth did that come from?'

Carl grinned, his good humour restored. 'Francisca brought it down while we were diving. I knew you'd want some lunch when you came ashore. Coffee will be served on the terrace, when we go back.'

He talked about diving during their picnic, then lapsed into silence. Lisa, still enchanted by the new underwater world she had discovered, was content to sit in the shade, trying to recall everything she had seen, trying to hold the memory close. Once she glanced at Carl, who was sprawled on the sand, and saw that he was looking at the bay, his face blank, his eyes half closed.

After a while he got up and waded into the sea without looking at her. She followed him, and they swam out beyond the bay to the open sea. From there, the bay could hardly be seen, and the white house on the hill gleamed from among a nest of trees. It reminded Lisa of the magazine photograph of Rachel, her flawless beauty nestled within soft white fur.

She stopped following Carl and floated for a while, suddenly aware of how tired she was after her dive. Then she swam slowly back to the beach, moving through the water with easy, leisurely strokes.

She had been dried by the sun before Carl appeared at the mouth of the bay. He swam down the centre of the enclosed stretch of water with strong, smooth strokes that scarcely disturbed the surface, his powerful arms rising and falling with the precision of an engine, his black head almost submerged.

As he stood upright in the shallows and began to wade towards her sunlight covered his brown wet body from head to foot. He was like a knight in a suit of closely-fitting bronze armour, each fine, strong sheet of metal shaping the breadth of his shoulders, the muscular planes of his chest, narrowing to a flat, hard stomach and long legs. His brief yellow trunks enhanced the appearance of a golden figure, and as he walked through the final ripples droplets thrown up by his passing sparkled like jewels. Drips of water from his wet, curly hair glittered in the sun as they fell to his shoulders and rolled down his chest.

He looked magnificent, and as he came to her Lisa was aware of a tingle of excitement. It was such a strong and frightening feeling that she

dragged her gaze away from his, picking up a
pebble at random and studying it to hide the
flush she was certain must have stained her face.

'Tired?' his deep voice asked. She had to look
up, her eyes travelling from the feet planted on
the rock before her, up the length of his legs, his
body, to his shoulders and then his face. He
seemed to be quite unaware of the turmoil she
felt within herself.

'A bit.'

'Let's go back to the house. You could do with
a hot drink.'

By the time they reached the terrace Lisa had
recovered from what she could only think of as a
bout of silly, girlish behaviour. They put the
diving equipment on the terrace and Carl took
her into the house, along a brown-tiled hallway
lined with doors. He opened one of the doors and
ushered her into a bedroom that looked over the
gardens at the side of the house.

'You can use this room—the bathroom's
through here. Come out on to the terrace when
you're ready.' His dark eyes swept over the
blouse and slacks she had picked up as they
crossed the terrace. 'You could do with something
cooler to wear.'

He threw open the doors of a wardrobe that
took up one wall, and pulled out a soft wisp of
turquoise that seemed to float in his fingers.
'Wear this. It belongs to your sister.'

She took it from him. 'It's Rachel's?'

He understood immediately. His lips twisted in
an amused smile. 'Oh, don't alarm yourself, little

sister——' there was a return to the mockery of before, but this time without anger. 'Rachel and I weren't sharing the same bedroom. She left it here during a photographic session. It's all very respectable.'

She flushed, then remembered, 'My bag—I left it in the beach buggy. I'll just——'

'I'll bring it,' he said, and went out, closing the door behind him.

The bedroom was large and beautifully furnished. The bathroom, leading from it, was tiled in apple green flecked with black and gold. Lisa slipped her swimsuit off, stepped into the shower and let the warm water flow over her face, hair and body. As she was towelling herself dry she realised that she was enjoying the day after all. Perhaps Carl wasn't such a strange choice for Rachel to make. He certainly had money, which mattered a lot to Rachel. She envied her sister, who might one day be the mistress of this magnificent house.

Her bag was lying on the wide bed beside the turquoise dress when she went back into the bedroom. Lisa rubbed her hair vigorously with the towel, then brushed it out before getting dressed. Rachel's turquoise dress settled over her shoulders like snowflakes, soft and loose-fitting, with a faint echo of Rachel's perfume clinging to its folds. It was calf-length, a simple dress with narrow shoulder straps and a deep, rounded neckline that would display Rachel's perfect body beautifully. On Lisa, it revealed just enough cleavage to give her a demure, youthful air, she thought, studying herself in the mirror and marvelling at the difference the wearer could make to clothes. Rachel's clothes were always part of her, selected to offset her looks and her personality. On Lisa, clothes tended to be just clothes, with no subtle, seductive promises of the body they covered. She ran her fingers through her damp hair, lifted it to let the air reach the roots, then let it fall back into place.

She put on a faint touch of lipstick, then walked barefoot through the hall and on to the terrace. The turquoise dress swirled pleasantly about her as she moved and her body felt free and lithe beneath it.

Francisca was setting out coffee on a shaded table. A jug of iced orange and a bowl of fruit were already on the table. She smiled, nodded, and went silently back into the house. Carl was nowhere to be seen, and the diving equipment had gone.

Lisa poured out a glass of orange, sipped at it, then put it down and went to the wrought-iron railing edging the terrace. Below, the swimming pool was a cool blue oblong. Beyond it flowers tumbled down to the trees, and then came the beach, about half of it in view. It was a paradise on earth, and she envied Rachel once more, realising as she did so that her sister would probably not even want to spend much time on Minorca.

She walked, her bare feet making no sound and the dress floating like a cloud around her, to the huge stone pot in one corner of the terrace. It held a tall, thick bush with dark green leaves and large, delicate white flowers. The scent of the flowers was sweet but not cloying, their petals cool and soft against her palm as she held them and stared down into their golden hearts.

'Aren't you going to come and have some coffee?' Carl asked. Lisa turned swiftly, began to release the flower she had cupped in her hand, then stopped as he ordered sharply, 'No! Wait there!'

She stared at him. 'What do you mean, wait here?'

He was on his way into the house. 'Just wait there. Don't move!' he tossed the words over his shoulder. Before she could decide whether he had lost his senses, or whether he really meant it he was back, a camera in his hand.

'Right—now stand back there, against the bush, just where you were when I spoke to you.'

'Carl, honestly——' she started to move towards him. 'I'm not one of your models!'

'Do as you're told!' he snapped, and she froze, one bare foot poised above the flagstones, then slowly drew it back. He didn't sound like a man who would tolerate disobedience.

Once again he was the complete professional, absorbed in his work. And she was only the subject—first a skin-diving pupil, now a model. She waited while he prowled back and forth across the terrace like a restless tiger in its cage, glancing over his shoulder to check the sun, fiddling with the light meter in his other hand.

'Turn towards the flowers—shoulders slightly

back. Touch that flower, just as you did earlier—
don't grab at it, just touch it!' he barked at her.
'Now—chin up a bit, look at me, but keep your
body turned towards the bush. For God's sake,
girl, relax! I'm not going to rape you.'

'I know,' she murmured. 'I'm not your type.'
If he heard her, he ignored the remark.

'Turn your head just a little away from me—
chin down a fraction—keep your eyes on me!'
She followed him obediently with her eyes as he
roved round the terrace, studying her from
different angles, a dissatisfied frown dragging his
well-shaped brows together. He had put on the
brown and gold shirt and brown trousers again.
The shirt was unbuttoned to the waist to show a
gold chain resting against his chest. He had only
towelled his hair, leaving it uncombed, and it
curled in damp tendrils round his lean-featured,
serious face. Lisa found it very easy to keep her
eyes on him.

He gave a little grunt of satisfaction below his
breath as he found the right angle, then the
camera was lowered again and his frown
deepened. For a moment he stood still, head on
one side, half-closed dark eyes studying her face
feature by feature. Then his eyes widened, the
frown disappeared.

'I know what's wrong. You need to come
alive.'

'How can——'

'Be quiet!' he said tersely, and in three long
strides he had covered the area between them,
dropping the camera and light meter on to a

chair. Before she realised what he was going to do, he had pulled one narrow strap from her shoulder, his fingers cool on her sun-warmed skin.

Lisa opened her mouth to protest, but at that moment Carl took her gently, firmly into his arms, and his lips closed on hers.

Her reaction was to draw back, but he held her firmly against his body, as his mouth moulded itself to hers, seeking, claiming, demanding—and exploring, as her lips parted and she submitted to him. One hand shaped the nape of her neck, beneath her still-damp hair, the other spread across her back.

His kiss, his nearness, brought indescribable pleasure. She had never known what it was like to be kissed like that. She felt his heart beating steadily, strongly, against her breast, and her own heart fluttering in answer. Her arms, tensed to push him away, relaxed and crept round him. Her fingers sank deep into the tight wet black curls at the back of his head. Her whole body, after the first shock of his embrace, answered him, reaching out to him, wanting him—and then she was alone, standing by the flowering bush, dazed and trembling, and Carl was walking back to pick up the camera.

He wheeled to face her again. 'Now, just stand the way I told you to before——' his voice was crisp, matter-of-fact; his eyes, in the instant before he raised the camera, studied her with professional expertise that had no personal interest at all. If their kiss had stirred him he gave no sign of it. 'That's much better. Here we go—just keep your eyes on me and do as I say.'

He moved from one part of the terrace to another, stepping on to a chair to get height, or going down on one knee to get a low-level shot. He even stepped from a chair to the iron railing that edged the terrace, balancing there without any apparent trouble as he took photographs then springing down, while Lisa, her heart in her mouth, waited for him to topple over on to the paving round the pool below. His voice rattled out instructions as the shutter clicked and clicked, over and over again. In a dream she followed his orders, turning, smiling, frowning, looking up, looking down—and all the time the memory of his kiss and his arms about her seemed more real than the present.

'Okay.' At last he put the camera down and dropped on to a chair, reaching for the coffee-pot, which stood over a low flame. 'Come and have some coffee—you've earned it.'

'Why did you do that?'

He raised an eyebrow as she sat opposite him, pulling the strap of the dress back over her shoulder. 'Do what—kiss you? I told you, you needed to be brought to life. You were too—too reserved.'

'I meant, why did you take the photographs?' Her knees were still weak, and she was grateful for the opportunity to sit down.

'Because I can't resist taking pictures of beautiful women.'

'I'm not beautiful,' she protested.

'You were, in that dress, standing by the flowers.' Carl passed a cup across the table to her, poured coffee for himself.

'But Rachel's the beauty of our family.'

'She has a sophisticated beauty—yes. A rich beauty. You have good bone structure, good colouring. Too stiff, though. That's why I had to bring the passion in you to the surface.'

'I'm not the passionate type,' Lisa said sharply—too sharply. He put his cup down, looked up at her thoughtfully, then smiled.

'You think not? Little sister, every woman has passion. You certainly have it. Perhaps you've never been kissed properly before, eh?'

She spooned sugar into her cup, and was surprised to see that her hands were steady. 'Do you always kiss your models?'

He looked amused. 'Only the beautiful ones. And if you're angling for a compliment, I can assure you that kissing you was a pleasure. Quite definitely, little sister—a pleasure!'

CHAPTER FIVE

THE laughter in Carl's eyes was more than Lisa could cope with. Confused, she stared down at her coffee, at the spoon that seemed to be stirring the brown liquid of its own volition. Then she released the spoon as Carl's finger tipped her chin up so that she had to look at him again. This time he looked surprised.

'What's wrong? Don't tell me you're not used to being kissed? How old are you, little sister?'

'Twenty.'

The eyebrows rose. 'And you still get upset when a man dares to kiss you?' he asked in mock horror.

She drew back, releasing herself from his touch. 'Of course I've been kissed! But not——' she stopped abruptly. But not in that way, she thought. Not as though I was the only woman in the world, being kissed by the only man in the world, for the first time in the history of the world——

'Not——?' he probed gently.

'Not by the man who's going to marry my sister.'

His hand, still stretched out towards her, was withdrawn, and his face darkened. It was his turn to stare down at the table. 'The man who was going to marry your sister,' he corrected this last. 'She changed her mind, remember?'

'She didn't change her mind—she didn't say she wasn't going to marry you! I know Rachel——'

'And you think I should wait for her, is that it? You might know your sister, but you don't know me!' The cold, sharp note was back in his voice.

'If you love her——'

'If she loved me she wouldn't have gone off to Paris!'

'That's not fair! You know how important her work is to her. She's spent years getting to the top in her profession, and this Paris assignment must have been important to her. She would have stayed here if it wasn't.'

'So you don't think that marriage is important?' his eyes were stormy.

'I didn't say that. I wanted to explain how Rachel must have felt.'

'There is no need for you to make explanations for Rachel. And it won't make any difference. My wife must always put me first,' he said flatly.

'I see. Well, that might suit Spanish women, but it doesn't go down very well with the rest of us,' Lisa assured him.

Carl laughed. 'Equality? I know all about that, little sister. As I said, my wife must always put me first, and I will always put her first. I won't take second place to any career.'

'You may have to, where Rachel's concerned.'

'Then don't you think it's as well that we are not going to marry after all?'

'You can't say that without talking it over with her first. You love her—why else did you want to marry her in the first place?'

'Love her?' He got up abruptly, walked to the railing, and leaned on it, staring down over the garden to the sea beyond. Then he turned. 'Love her? I'm beginning to wonder, now. Perhaps——' he spread his arms wide, and the sun glinted on the gold chain at his brown throat. 'Perhaps I only desired her. Oh, Lisa——' his voice was faintly amused again, the anger gone, 'I've shocked you. You're so easily shocked.'

She couldn't look at him, couldn't meet those clear dark eyes, that quizzical mouth. 'Not really. I'm just not used to clever conversation. I don't mix with the same people you and Rachel are used to.'

'You think we're clever? My dear Lisa, we can't even plan out a simple thing like a quiet wedding without getting into a mess. We're not clever, Rachel and I. Perhaps we're fools.'

When she remained silent, he returned to the table, sat opposite her, and reached out to remove the coffee cup from her hand, retaining her fingers in a light but firm grasp.

'Talk to me about love, little sister,' he said. His voice, with its faint soft accent, was like dark brown velvet surrounding her, caressing her, bewitching her——

'I can't,' she said abruptly. 'I've never been in love!' She wanted to get up and move away from him, but the hand over hers kept her prisoner.

'What do you imagine it to be like?' he suggested gently. 'If you were in love, if you really cared for a man, what would it be like?'

'I'd—I'd want to be with him, make him

happy——' Lisa stopped, realising that she was being led into a trap.

'You see?' His voice was triumphant and a tremor ran through the fingers holding hers. 'You wouldn't go rushing off to Paris, would you? You'd want to stay with him. I agree with you, Lisa—that is love. I'm really a very conservative man. I believe in marriage. I want,' said Carl slowly 'to love, and honour, and cherish my woman.'

As she watched their intertwined hands on the tabletop Lisa sensed that tingle of excitement again. She was still shellshocked by his unexpected kiss, she told herself severely. It was time she pulled herself together.

Carl captured one of her fingers, then another, then a third, as he repeated, half to himself, 'To love her—honour her—cherish her——' He lifted the three imprisoned fingers to his lips, brushed a kiss across them, then returned them to her side of the table.

'But not,' he added firmly 'to the extent of waiting around while she goes flying off to Paris!'

She drew her hand into her lap. 'It's time I got back to the apartment, Carl.'

'But I've already told Francisca that we'll dine here.' He stopped her as she started to protest. 'It's all arranged. She doesn't often have the opportunity to cook for anyone nowadays, and she's looking forward to it. You have no other plans for this evening, have you?'

'Well, I—no.'

'It's all arranged, then,' he repeated. 'Now I

have some paper-work to deal with, if you'll excuse me. Perhaps you'd like to rest, or take a look around the place.' He seemed to have tired of the cat and mouse game, to her relief.

It was soothing to be left alone, free of his vibrant, disturbing presence. Lisa walked down past the little swimming pool, through the gardens, and into the trees. When she looked back the house gleamed in the sunlight like a pearl set among the brilliant colours of the garden. Before her the sea could be seen shimmering between branches and leaves. She explored the beach and the garden, then went back to the bedroom Carl had set aside for her use. It was pleasant to get out of the glare of the sun, though the strong heat of the day was beginning to diminish as evening approached. The bed was soft and inviting, and after a moment's hesitation Lisa took off the turquoise dress and lay down to rest, pulling the light apple-green sheet over her.

She woke suddenly without any apparent drifting upwards from her deep sleep, and found herself staring into Carl's eyes. He was standing by the bed, thumbs hooked into his belt, watching her. She reached instinctively for the sheet, which only just covered her breasts, and pulled it protectively up to her shoulders. His eyes followed the gesture, and in the last rays of the sun, shining through the long windows on to his lean face, she saw his lips curve in a smile.

'Amost time for dinner.'

She started to sit up, then sank back on to the pillows, still clutching the sheet.

'I won't be a moment.' She tried to make her

voice as dismissive as possible. He picked up the
turquoise dress from the back of a chair and
tossed it on to the bed, within her reach.

'Wear this again, it suits you. The dining
room's the second door on the left.'

She waited until the door clicked shut behind
him before she moved. Ten minutes later,
dressed and lightly made up, her hair brushed
into shining submission, she opened the door at
the end of the hall and found herself in a square,
low-ceilinged room with most of the floor space
taken up by a huge polished oval table. Two
places had been set near each other at one end of
the table, and the light, supplied by candles set in
heavy, ornate silver candlesticks, gleamed softly
on cutlery, glasses and china.

Carl, his hair neatly brushed, his shirt
buttoned and with a vivid blue cravat tucked into
the open neck, was by the large, carved sideboard
opening a bottle of wine. Francisca was placing a
soup tureen on the table. As Lisa went in, the
older woman smiled warmly at her and went out
of the room through a door in the rear wall.

'Did you sleep well?' Carl brought the opened
bottle to the table and pulled out a chair for Lisa.
He was the perfect host as he served her with
delicious chilled soup, poured wine, made sure that
everything was to her taste. Even in casual clothes,
he looked as though he belonged to the opulent
background of the house. Lisa was beginning to
realise that Carl had the knack of blending into any
background he chose. Francisca moved about the
table as they ate, clearing dishes, setting the next

course, exchanging comments in her own tongue
with Carl as she worked.

'It's a pity you can't talk to each other, you'd
like her. She's delighted to have the opportunity
to cook a decent meal for once,' he said when she
had left them.

Although she hadn't been able to follow what
they said Lisa had seen clearly that there was an
easy familiarity, a strong affection, between Carl
and Francisca.

'Have you known her long?' she asked.

'She first came to work on our farm when I
was a child. I can't remember life without
Francisca.'

Lisa looked about the room, most of it hidden
in the shadows beyond the golden pool of light
from the candles, then she looked at Carl in his
high-backed chair, a glass of ruby-red wine in
one hand. 'It's a beautiful house—and it's so
large!'

'Not really. Most of the space is taken up by
the terracing and the balcony,' he said carelessly.
'As for this——' he indicated the huge table
where they sat, 'my parents had a lot of children,
and my father wanted to make sure that there was
always room for us to be together. But we haven't
been together for a long time,' his face darkened.
'Not since my mother died, and my father moved
to Ibiza.'

'Your family doesn't live on this island now?'

'Only one brother. Some live on the mainland,
some abroad. It was never the same after my
father sold the farmland.'

'Tell me about the farm.'

His face seemed to be carved from fine, rich wood in the candlelight. 'You wouldn't be interested.'

'I would.'

He moved one shoulder in a slight shrug. 'Just tell me when you want me to stop talking, then.'

Drugged by the sea and the sun and the splendour about her, bewitched by his deep voice and its attractive English, fascinated by his memories, Lisa was content to sit and listen during the meal as Carl talked about the old farm where he had been raised, about his hard-working parents, his mother's illness. She heard bitterness creep into his voice as he went on to tell her about his father's decision to sell the farm and its land and use the money to build a fine house where Carl's mother would be free to rest and recover.

'While I was working in England,' Carl said, anger in his voice. 'It was done before I knew about it. Of course, the developers were glad to pay well for the land and the bulldozers had torn the heart out of the farm before I got back home. All I had was a strip of land by the sea, where the apartment is now.'

'Your brothers didn't want to farm?'

He shook his head, staring at a candle-flame with fierce concentration. 'Only me—and as the youngest member of my family I wasn't consulted.'

'You mean that you wanted to become a farmer

in your father's place?' It was yet another surprise from this strange man.

He laughed shortly. 'You see? Nobody believes that a man who has once left the island would be content to come back and settle down. But I would have—willingly. I still would.'

'You could buy another farm.'

When he looked at her the candle-flame's reflection danced deep in his dark eyes. 'I will only farm land that belonged to my family. As a matter of fact——' then he stopped, shrugged.

'What happened after the farm was sold?'

'My mother died.' His mouth twisted briefly. 'The fine house my father built couldn't save her after all. He didn't want to live here without her, so he moved to a cottage in Ibiza. Selling the farm was an unnecessary sacrifice after all. The others—they married, moved away. I don't see them often. The heart was gone from the farm, and when my mother died the heart was gone from the family. Nobody could save it.'

'I'd like to meet your father,' Lisa said impulsively, and he looked surprised.

'He's only a farmer. A man of rock, difficult to know and to understand.'

'I'd still like to meet him, some day. Does Rachel know him?' She remembered what Mike had said about Carl's family. 'Was your father invited to your wedding?'

His voice deepened to a harsh note. 'I wasn't invited to take part in a family conference about the land. My marriage has nothing to do with my family!'

'You mean that they wouldn't approve of you marrying someone from outside the island?' she asked boldly, and he turned angry dark eyes on her.

'I mean that it is not their business!' he snapped, pushing his chair back abruptly and getting to his feet. She watched his broad back as he went to the sideboard, the rigid set of his shoulders, and knew that she had pried too much. But when he came back to the table the anger had gone, and his handsome face was expressionless.

'These are for you——' he swept cutlery and glasses out of the way, and tossed a sheaf of glossy photographs across the table in a fan.

Lisa picked up the print nearest her—and gasped.

She was looking at the photograph of a girl—a lovely girl with a mass of rich chestnut curls clustered round a small, neat-featured face dominated by wide hazel eyes shot with gold lights. The eyes were fringed by thick dark lashes and the model's lips, slightly parted as she gazed into the camera, were full and red. Her long slender neck and rounded shoulders were bare, with the perfect sheen of a pearl. The soft curves of her breasts could just be glimpsed above the line of a turquoise dress, the perfect foil for her colouring. One raised hand gently cupped a flawless white flower. The girl was demure, tantalising, with an appealing blend of youth and maturity that caught the eye and the imagination.

The photograph fell from Lisa's fingers. She picked up another, then another. Whatever the pose, the model retained that bewitching freshness blended with the slightly sophisticated hint of first ripening. It was a face that would arouse interest in a crowd.

The final photograph was of the model looking into the camera from above, her glowing hair tumbling over her forehead, her eyes dreamy and trusting, her lips shaped as though she was about to speak.

Lisa felt dazed as she put the print down and lifted her eyes to Carl's face. He was leaning forward in his chair, elbows on the table, watching her reaction closely.

'Well, little sister?'

'But-but I look beautiful!'

'I told you you were. Now do you believe me?'

'I don't really look like that. It's the photography——'

'All you needed——' his eyes moved over her hair, her face, her throat, her mouth, and she found herself holding her breath, '—was that kiss to bring you to life. I only take the pictures, little sister. I can't create the beauty. It has to be there, waiting to be brought to life.'

His gaze caught and held hers and she was relieved when Francisca came in with a tray of coffee and broke the spell that refused to let her eyes leave Carl's.

The woman smilingly exchanged a few words with him before leaving the room. He took liqueur glasses and a bottle of golden liquid from the beautifully-carved sideboard.

Lisa wasn't fond of liqueurs, but was surprised, when she cautiously sipped the contents of her glass, to find that it was delicious. The sweetness was underlaid with a sharp tang that took away the syrupy effect.

Carl nodded approval when he saw her surprise. 'I thought you'd like it. A friend of mine makes it.' He poured out coffee for them both.

Outside, the night sky was brushed with colours shading from crimson to palest pink, streaked with pale grey. Now that it was getting darker the candlelight within the room seemed to be stronger, bathing them both in a pool of gold that enhanced Carl's good looks. Lisa felt she was caught in a fairy-tale—but someone else's story, she reminded herself swiftly. A magic world that was meant for Rachel, not her.

The recollection that she was just visiting Rachel's story made her ask bluntly, without stopping to think first, 'Why are you being so charming?'

Carl's eyes widened and he almost gaped at her before he recovered and said lightly, 'Because I have a naturally charming nature.'

'I didn't notice it when we first met—or at the harbour yesterday.'

A muscle jumped in his jaw. 'Everyone can make mistakes. I thought—wrongly—that Rachel had persuaded you to help her in some way. Now I feel that you've been deceived, just as I was.'

'Deceived?'

When he didn't answer, didn't look at her, she went on, 'But why give up your entire day to me—why all this?' she indicated the table, the remnants of the meal, the wine and candles.

He took a deep breath, then looked up at her. 'Because I wanted to be with someone today. I didn't want to be alone.'

The thought of Carl being afraid on his own struck her as funny, but when she began to laugh he didn't join in. Instead his mouth tightened and he stared down into his liqueur glass.

'Does that amuse you?' he queried. 'Have you never wanted company?'

'Often. But I can't imagine you needing to be with someone, particularly a stranger like me.'

'You've forgotten, haven't you?' His voice was harsh.

'Forgotten what?'

'That today was to have been my wedding day!' he rapped across the table at her, and Lisa stared at him, appalled by her own indifference. She had forgotten. All at once she felt a surge of compassion for him. The man who had everything and who hadn't wanted to be alone on his wedding day. She reached across the table, covered his hand with her own, then pulled her hand back as he recoiled, getting to his feet.

'You don't have to give me your pity!' he snapped. 'I only asked for your company!'

'Rachel's going to come back to you. I know she will!'

He turned, the liqueur bottle in one hand, his newly refilled glass in the other.

'When she does—if she does, you can tell her not to bother getting in touch with me. I'm no longer in the market,' he said cruelly, and seated himself again.

The silence between them was so long that Lisa thought it would never end. Then, just when she was about to ask him to take her back to the flat, he said, in a conversational voice, 'We've talked about Rachel, and about me, but not about you. I thought women always wanted to talk about themselves.'

She wondered, briefly, how many women he had known, and how well he had known them, before he met Rachel.

'There's nothing to talk about,' she shrugged.

'What about your boy-friend?'

'Paul? Oh, he's——' then she stopped abruptly. 'How did you find out about him?'

Carl looked amused. 'An attractive woman always has a special man in her life.'

'Paul isn't special.' Even as she said it, she realised that it was true. Once she had thought that Paul was going to be special. Now she knew he never would be.

'You'll meet the right man soon, little sister.'

'I wish you wouldn't call me that!'

'What is it that Rachel calls you? Mouse? Why?'

'My name's Melissa,' she explained reluctantly. 'When I was born, Rachel couldn't say it, so she changed it to Mouse, and it stuck. I hate it, but I suppose it fits.'

'Does it?' His dark eyebrows edged up again.

'Brown hair—hazel eyes. I'm mousy, ordinary.'

'I don't think so.' His gaze travelled over her hair, her mouth, her throat, then over her body. 'Melissa.' She had never realised, until she heard it spoken in his deep, husky voice, what a lovely name it was. 'It suits you.'

She laughed, a trifle shakily. 'It reminds me of a princess waiting in a tower for the prince to come along and——' she stopped on the verge of saying, 'kiss her awake,' and changed it to '—and rescue her.'

'Then I hope your prince arrives very soon, Melissa.' Carl lifted his glass in a toast to her, then drained the last drops, his strong throat working easily as he swallowed. 'Would you like more coffee?'

'No, thank you. It's getting late—and I don't want to give Francisca any more work at this time of night.'

'I was going to make it myself,' Carl said casually. 'Francisca lives in the village a mile away. She left for home ages ago. We're quite alone now.'

CHAPTER SIX

ALL at once Lisa was aware of the bulk of the house, silent and empty, apart from the two of them. The last of the sunset was fading beyond the windows and the trees were dark shadows, blending into the sky.

'I must get back to the apartment,' she said quickly, and Carl laughed.

'Don't worry, little sister, I'm not going to take advantage of you,' he said, a teasing note in his voice as he got to his feet. 'I'll drive you back. Just leave these things where they are,' he added carelessly as she began to gather the coffee cups and liqueur glasses together.

'I don't mind—it'll save Francisca extra work in the morning——' Lisa knew that she was making a fool of herself, that Rachel would have swept from the room without giving the table a second glance. But Carl stood by the door. She would have to pass him to get out, and the realisation that they were quite alone made it difficult to think straight. She moved to the sideboard, picked up a tray that lay there, and began to stack the cups and glasses on to it.

'Francisca is quite capable——' Irritation filtered through his voice. She didn't dare look up at him.

'I'll take them to the kitchen,' she said.

'Do you have to be such a domesticated little mouse?' The studied cruelty in the words stung, but she couldn't give in now. She moved towards the door, the tray clutched in her hands as though it offered some form of protection—against what, she didn't know. Carl stepped back, away from the open door.

'I-I hate to leave a table in a mess——'

'How very English of you!' he mocked. 'Third door on your right. If you want to wash up, I'm sure you'll find an apron that fits.'

Crimson-cheeked, unable to meet his eyes, she went into the hall, fumbled for the handle of the kitchen door.

'Be careful——' said Carl from right behind her, 'there's a step down——'

She hadn't realised that he had followed her along the hall. In her haste to get away from him she didn't take in his words properly. Balancing the tray in one hand, she opened the door with the other, stepped forward, and fell down the step just inside the kitchen. The loaded tray crashed to the floor with a thunderous noise that set her ears ringing. The light flashed on and Lisa was scooped without ceremony into Carl's arms.

'Are you all right?'

She clutched at his shoulders for support, still dazed. 'I-I think so. I just got a fright.'

'That was a stupid thing to do! Why can't you listen to me? I told you to leave things alone—I told you to be careful——'

'Don't shout at me!' She pulled herself free, fright and humiliation combining to form rage.

'What a crazy place to put a step! How on earth is a stranger to know it's there?'

'A stranger should mind her own business! And for heaven's sake, leave it!' he added sharply as she bent to gather broken glass and china from the blue-tiled floor.

'I can't leave the place in a mess like this!'

He caught her arms again, pulled her upright to face him. 'Yes, we can. Are you sure you're all right? You could have broken your ankle, do you realise that.'

'Of course I haven't broken it! What do you think I am—one of your fragile little models? Let me go, Carl, I'll have to sweep up this broken glass!'

'And while you're about it you'll probably manage to cut yourself and bleed to death, won't you?' he wanted to know, the anger gone from his voice. When she finally allowed herself to look up at him she saw laughter creeping into his eyes. His fury was like a summer storm—arriving without warning and departing as unexpectedly.

His amusement only fanned her own anger. 'You think it's all very funny, don't you? You think I'm some sort of joke!'

'No, I don't.' He tried hard to subdue the grin that had begun to spread over his face, but didn't quite manage to straighten out his features. 'What does it matter if a few glasses got broken? Come on, I'll take you home.'

'Not until I've cleared up this mess.'

'You're nagging, little sister,' he said solemnly.

'I don't nag, I only——' Lisa stopped as she

saw the grin widen again. 'Why won't you ever take me seriously?' she asked, exasperated.

One eyebrow lifted slightly. 'You really want me to take you seriously? Well, if you insist, little sister——'

Before she realised what he meant, his lips were on hers, his arms sliding about her. She fought against him without much effect.

'That was what I call quite serious,' he said when the kiss ended. 'Now, if you want me to take you very seriously, I can——'

She put her hands against his chest, pushed herself back to glare up into his face. 'Carl, you're behaving like a——'

'Shut up,' he ordered, then kissed her again, a demanding kiss that sent her senses reeling. Without realising it, she stopped struggling, slid her hands across his broad back. When, at last, she murmured a protest and tried to draw away Carl swept her off her feet and into his arms, his lips still holding hers.

She felt herself being carried up the step that had caused all the trouble, then along the hall. His lips released hers, leaving her too breathless to speak. When he set her down in the room she had used earlier he kissed her once more, briefly, fiercely, then straightened up, his arms still about her.

She could hear him breathing quickly, could see his eyes glittering down at her in the dusk. But there wasn't enough light from the windows to let her make out his expression.

His voice was husky when he finally broke

the silence. 'Have I shocked you again? It was the only way to get you safely out of the kitchen. And now, little sister, isn't it time I took you home?'

He let his arms slacken about her, but didn't release her completely. She knew that she could, and should, step away from him, and he would make no attempt to stop her. But there was a new tension holding them together, a new awareness of each other. Something in Carl's complete stillness as he loomed over her told her that he sensed it too. They stood in a silence that was filled with questions and answers, words that were not spoken aloud yet clamoured in their ears.

'If—that's what you want,' Carl said at last, without moving. Lisa closed her eyes briefly, but she couldn't blot him out. He was still there, his very presence touching every nerve end in her body and setting up a glow that enveloped her from head to foot. She opened her eyes again, staring up into his shadowy face.

It would take only one word, she knew, and he would move to the light switch, put it on, then go out and start the engine while she changed out of Rachel's turquoise dress and gathered her things together. Just one word.

Slowly, as slowly as she had moved when she was swimming underwater with him, she reached up and touched his face, her fingertips tracing a line from the corner of his mouth to his temple, her palm cupping the hard planes of his cheek. She heard him draw in his breath with a slight sigh, then he reached for her and drew her towards him, hungrily seeking her lips.

Neither of them said anything when his mouth finally left hers. His kisses fluttered tantalisingly over her cheek before he buried his face in her hair. His tongue gently caressed the line of her ear, and the lobe was caught between his teeth for a moment. Then his lips moved to the hollow between her chin and neck, from there to her throat and over the curve of her shoulder. For the second time that day he pushed one turquoise strap from her shoulder, but this time his fingers remained there for a moment, caressing her skin before giving way to his impatient mouth. The dress whispered softly in the quiet room as Lisa felt herself being lifted into his arms, carried across the floor, then lowered gently into the bed.

Part of her mind told her that this moment was madness, but the past and the future seemed to break up, become filmy and unimportant. Carl, his hair soft against her face, his kisses burning her skin, his hands teasing a response from her body, was the only reality for her.

She sensed the deep need in him and answered it, responding to his blend of passion and tenderness with ease. She allowed herself to become totally absorbed in him, and in the world they had created together.

He tossed his blue cravat aside and she felt the skin of his chest slip smoothly against her shoulder as he bent over her, his lips in her hair. Then his mouth moved back to hers and she wrapped her arms about him, drawing him close, sharing his passion and intensity.

Somewhere, far away, a car engine hummed, then stopped. A door banged. Lisa heard, but paid no heed. But the door-knocker was a clamour that refused to be shut out. Carl lifted his head briefly, then looked down at her in the darkness of the room, his breath warm on her cheek.

'Pay no attention.'

But the spell had been broken. The angry clamour of the villa door-knocker had managed to intrude, and couldn't be ignored. 'They must know you're here—whoever it is.'

'So?' he tried to push her back, gently, as she struggled to sit up. 'Does it matter?'

'Carl, you'll have to go and see who it is. We can't leave someone standing on the doorstep!'

'I can——' he said, and the note in his voice sent a shiver of pleasure through her. It would have been so easy to give way to that note, to sink back on the soft bed and put her arms about him again. But it was too late; common sense was returning.

'Carl—please——'

He got up reluctantly, smoothing his hair back with impatient fingers as he went to the door. He paused there, silhouetted against the dim light that burned in the hall.

'Don't go away—I won't be long——' his whisper floated across the room to her before he went out, closing the door softly behind him.

The wonder of their sudden closeness went with him. Her skin still tingled, her lips carried the imprint of his kisses, but all at once, without Carl, Lisa came back to reality with a jarring thud.

What had she been thinking of, letting her sister's fiancé make love to her? And the blame didn't lie solely with Carl, she realised miserably. She had thrown herself at him, behaved like a complete fool. She got up, searching for the sandals she had kicked off, fumbling for the light switch.

The mirror showed her that her hair was tumbled, her face flushed, her eyes enormous. She turned to look for her bag, then stopped short as she heard a woman's voice in the hall. Lisa immediately thought of Rachel, and before she had time to reason things out her hand was on the door-knob and the door was open.

Carl was leaning against the wall by the closed front door, arms folded and face dark as he listened to the woman who stood with her back towards Lisa, bombarding him with a torrent of Spanish. As Lisa appeared he automatically glanced up and his visitor spun round, alerted.

She was small, slender, dark and very beautiful. She wore a beautifully cut trouser suit of a gold silky material over a low-necked white blouse. Rings sparkled on her red-tipped little hands.

She drew in her breath with an audible hiss as she saw Lisa. 'Señorita Maxwell?'

'Yes?' Lisa realised all at once that she must look terrible. She reached up to pull the dress strap firmly on to her shoulder, and the other two noticed the movement. Carl raised his eyes to the ceiling, sighed, and eased his broad shoulders free of the wall.

The woman advanced down the hall, her dark eyes flashing. 'Señorita, you will please go away at once!'

'Go——?'

'From this house, from this island, from Carlos!' The English wasn't good but the meaning was unmistakable. So was the hatred in her face as she stared up at Lisa.

Before she could say a word Carl had brushed past the visitor and was by her side, his arm about her. As she tried to step out of his embrace the hand he had draped over her shoulder tightened, holding her where she was.

'That's enough, Maria!' he said coldly, but the Spanish woman's eyes had drifted to a point beyond Lisa's head, her eyes widening and her lips parting. Lisa didn't have to turn and look to realise that the woman had seen the bedroom, the rumpled apple-green cover on the bed, visible from where Maria stood. Damning evidence—if she knew that the two of them were alone together in the house.

Then, with a shock, she heard Carl say above her head, 'You have no right to burst in here and speak like that to the woman I'm going to marry!'

'So——' Maria said in a hiss, switching her attention back to him, 'so it is true, what we heard when we arrived back on the island today?'

'Your spies didn't waste time, did they?' Carl countered.

'You really mean to marry this—this woman?' Maria's eyes blazed at Lisa and she found herself shrinking back against Carl, stunned by the sheer hatred in the other woman's look.

'Of course. We love each other—don't we, darling?'

Lisa forgot Maria for a moment, twisting to look up at him. 'Carl, what——'

His arm tightened, holding her so closely against him that she could scarcely breathe. 'Hush, darling, I'll deal with this,' he told her.

'And what about your family? Why didn't you consult them about it?' Maria flared at him.

Held tightly against Carl, Lisa was aware of the sudden tension in his lithe body, though his voice was even when he retorted, 'It has nothing to do with them.'

'Your marriage? Carlos, how can you do this to your father—to Eduardo!'

'Don't you mean—to you?' he asked, his voice suddenly vicious, and Maria's eyes narrowed, giving her the look of a wildcat preparing to spring.

'They didn't consult me when they sold my family's land——' he went on, 'so why should I consult them about my marriage?'

'So—you marry this Englishwoman just to teach them a lesson? Carlos, you're a fool!' She spat the words at him.

Tension rippled through his muscular frame again. 'You don't really know me, Maria, do you? We're marrying because we want to spend the rest of our lives together, don't we, my love? We

want to make each other happy—isn't that what
you said to me just this afternoon, darling?'

Short of kicking his shins, there was no way
that Lisa could break free. She could only stand
within his close embrace and fume silently.

'Carlos——' A new coaxing note crept into
Maria's voice, coating it in honey. 'Carlos, send
her away, and let's talk. We need to talk.'

'You and I? We haven't had anything to say
to each other for years. Goodnight, Maria.
Better get back home before Eduardo wonders
where you are—or does he know you're visiting
me?'

Her breath hissed between small white teeth
again, and her slim hands curved into wildcat
claws. Then she whirled away from them and
walked, straight-backed, out of the front door. As
soon as it slammed shut Lisa struggled against
Carl's restraining arm. He released her and she
ran to the door.

'Where do you think you're going?'

She turned, one hand on the handle. 'To
explain to her——'

Carl walked up the length of the hall and took
both her hands in his. There was laughter in the
dark eyes that looked down at her.

'To tell her what? That you aren't my fiancée?
That you're Rachel's sister? That we're just
having a quiet, very proper chat about the
wedding? With that sort of evidence?' He jerked
his head towards the open bedroom door. 'My
dear Lisa, you know what she thought, don't
you?' he said easily. 'And, being Maria, she won't

stop thinking it. Not if we were able to provide a roomful of witnesses in our own defence. Which, of course, we can't.'

CHAPTER SEVEN

'BUT we weren't——' Lisa stopped, colour flaming into her face.

'I know that. You know that. But Maria has a very suspicious mind.'

'Why did you have to tell her that I was Rachel?'

'I didn't. She thought that one out for herself. I was just going along with the idea to protect your honour,' Carl pointed out smoothly. 'After all, with that evidence——'

'Will you stop saying that!'

The corners of his mouth quirked. '—it was better to let her go on thinking you were Rachel, wasn't it? The lesser of the two evils.'

The car engine started up, roared away with a clashing of gears.

'And what if she ever meets Rachel?'

'That isn't very likely now, is it? And if she does, then I'm quite sure she'll keep her mouth shut, for her own sake. Eduardo probably thinks she's visiting a friend. He would be horrified if he knew that she had come here, alone and late at night, to see me.'

'Eduardo?' queried Lisa.

'My brother. Maria's his wife.'

Lisa stared up at him. 'Your sister-in-law?'

'You sound surprised.'

'I thought she——' she recalled the jealousy in Maria's lovely face as she surveyed the two of them. 'I thought she was a-a——'

'A lover?' Carl asked casually. 'She was, a long time ago, when we were all young and—foolish. But I wasn't interested in making it permanent, and Maria wanted marriage, money, respectability. So she married my brother. But even though she's got all she wants now, she doesn't like to think of anyone getting me—succeeding where she failed.'

'That's a rotten thing to say!'

'No, it's not. Maria's man-hungry, that's her trouble. She's not content with poor Eduardo, she wants me on a string as well. And she's not getting me.' He raised his eyebrows slightly. 'I think Maria learned tonight that Peeping Toms sometimes see more than they bargained for. In a few days I'll go and see them. I'll tell Eduardo that the marriage has been cancelled. That I decided——' he caught Lisa's eyes, smiled faintly, and changed it to '—that we decided it wouldn't work after all. How does that sound?'

A sudden thought occurred to Lisa. 'It sounds as though you had a double reason for letting Maria believe that I was Rachel.'

'What?' he frowned at her, puzzled.

'To protect my honour——' she spoke the words with heavy sarcasm, 'and to hide the fact that your fiancée's walked out on you. Something Maria hasn't heard yet, apparently. This is the perfect chance for you to save your face, isn't it?'

Fury swept into his eyes, and she instinctively took a step back, coming up against the wall, as he glared at her.

'You——!' he muttered between his teeth, then he got himself under control with a visible effort, his mouth twisted in a cold smile. 'You are like your sister after all. Very good at knowing how to hurt people.'

The contempt in his voice stung colour into her cheeks. 'Me? I'm just a beginner as far as you're concerned!' she threw at him. 'And now I'd like to go home, if you don't mind!'

'I'd be delighted!'

They glared at each other. In that moment Lisa hated him, and it was obvious that he felt the same way about her. The lovely day, the enchanted moments they had spent in each other's arms, the kiss on the terrace, had ceased to exist.

She flounced into the bedroom, slammed the door, and tore off the fragile turquoise dress, tossing it across the room. When she had put her own clothes on and gone back to the hall she saw Carl coming down the staircase, shrugging his broad shoulders into a crimson anorak.

'Here——' he held a black safari jacket out to her, thrusting it at her impatiently when she started to shake her head. 'Take it and put it on! It can get cold here at nights in September.'

He pushed past her into the dining room as she was fastening the jacket, and returned with the bundle of photographs. 'They're yours, take them.'

'I'd rather not!'

Anger danced across his face. 'Take them, damn you! People pay me a lot of money for my photographs—you should feel honoured!'

Lisa almost snatched them from his hand and crammed them into her bag without giving them a glance. She promised herself that she would destroy them as soon as she got back to the flat.

Carl opened the door without a word and Lisa walked past him, out of the villa.

The night sky was velvet, sequined with stars and fastened into place by a clear moon. But Lisa was in no mood to admire it. Carl drove fast, angrily, swinging the beach buggy round corners with the squeal of protesting tyres, speeding along flat, wide empty roads. He didn't speak to her, didn't look at her, even when the buggy stopped outside the apartment block.

Lisa scrambled down as soon as the vehicle came to a standstill, without waiting for Carl to move. He started to speak, but she ignored him, hurrying up the open staircase, fumbling with the wrought iron gate at the top. The buggy door slammed below, and she prayed that Carl was going to drive away, and wasn't following her.

She found her key, opened the door that led directly into the lounge, then stopped, her hand half extended towards the light switch. There was something different about the room, something familiar and yet unexpected. It was too dark to see anything clearly, and yet——

Then she identified it. A faint, well-known exotic scent that hung on the still air. Just as she realised what it meant the light flashed on, commanded by the switch beside the short hall leading to kitchen and bedrooms.

'Mouse,' said Rachel in a soft, sleep-drugged voice, 'darling, what on earth have you been up to?'

She stood just inside the lounge. She wore a white filmy nightgown that left very little to the imagination, and over it she was fastening a matching negligee edged with lace. Her face was clear of make-up, but her flushed cheeks and drowsy green eyes had a natural beauty that outshone her sophisticated daytime self. Tawny hair tumbled carelessly over her shoulders.

A smile curved her lovely mouth as she watched Lisa. 'Coming in at this hour of the night—not like my little Mouse at all,' she teased. 'You must be having a good time! But what on earth have you done to your hair, darling?'

Lisa put a hand to the waves that framed her face as she stepped into the room.

'Rachel! When did you get back?'

'About an hour ago. I was too tired to wait up for you,' her sister yawned. 'The flight was terrible, and I thought the taxi would never get here——'

The patio gate rattled; the door, which Lisa had left ajar, was thrown open.

'Don't ever walk away from me ag——' Then Carl saw Rachel and stopped short. He stood motionless, just inside the door, staring at her. Lisa had no time to analyse the expressions that flitted across his face as he stood there. His first reaction was surprise, but she was still trying to decide whether she had seen love or relief when his face went blank and his eyes were shuttered.

Then he said, 'Rachel!' and she told herself that nobody could make the name sound so special unless it was spoken with very deep feeling. For some reason her heart turned over and began to beat faster.

Rachel had no doubts at all about her reception.

'Carl! Oh, darling——' she seemed to swim across the room, the white negligee billowing around her. Lisa was surrounded by that exotic scent as her sister brushed past her, then Rachel was on tiptoe, kissing Carl, weaving shapely arms about his neck, tangling her fingers in his hair, drawing his head down to hers. Watching her, Lisa remembered what it felt like to touch that soft, thick black hair.

Carl made no attempt to hold Rachel. Instead, he let her lips claim his for a moment, then took her wrists and pulled her hands from his neck as he lifted his head. Her fingers spread as her imprisoned hands slid slowly over his shoulders and down on to his chest, slipping inside the open neck of his shirt. He held her wrists there, making no further attempt to push her away from him.

'Carl, how lovely to see you!'

'What the hell are you doing here?' he asked coolly. The safari jacket slipped from Lisa's shoulders and she tossed it on to a divan.

Rachel laughed. 'What do you think I'm doing here? I've come back for our wedding.'

'Then you're too late. Today was to have been our wedding day, but I had to cancel it. I couldn't get married without a bride, could I?' His voice took on a harsh note. Rachel freed one wrist from his grip and caught his hand, turning it so that she could see the dial of the handsome watch he wore.

'Actually, yesterday was to have been our wedding day. This is our wedding night,' she said throatily, and her fingers returned to caress the brown skin at the open neck of his shirt. 'But we can arrange another date, darling.'

'You expect me to say yes, Rachel, let's arrange to get married any day you feel like it?' he demanded fiercely, pushing her away. 'I'm not one of your empty-headed admirers!'

The sleepiness fled from her eyes and they flashed like emeralds. 'Don't talk to me like that, Carl!'

'I'll talk to you any way I like!' he said slowly, viciously. For a moment Lisa thought that he was going to attack her sister, but as she took a quick step forward, Carl pushed Rachel back, away from him.

'Carl, stop it!'

'You keep out of this!' he ordered without taking his eyes off Rachel.

'Look—Rachel came back, didn't she? She came back as soon as her work in Paris was finished—what more could you ask? She came back to you!'

He was balanced on his feet like a panther ready to spring.

'As soon as her work in Paris was finished?

You mean you really didn't know? All that wide-eyed innocence of yours was genuine?'

'Know what?'

Now he threw a swift glance at her, his eyes like frosted black glass. 'That there was no photographic session in Paris. That your sister made it all up so that she could get away from Minorca!'

There was a silence. Lisa stared at him, trying to make sense of what she had just heard. Even Rachel was taken aback, then her shoulders lifted in a faint shrug.

'I might have known you'd check up on me, darling. It's the sort of thing a male chauvinist like you would do, isn't it? Spying's so—so deceitful!'

'Not as deceitful as walking out on your fiancé—and your sister. Or didn't you think of that, Rachel? I don't suppose you would. Not a selfish, pampered kitten like you!'

She laughed shortly. 'I knew Lisa could take care of herself. And come to think of it——' she added, her brilliant eyes moving to Lisa, then back to Carl '—she seems to have been taking care of herself very well. Or should I say, getting you to do it for her?'

'Rachel——!' Lisa burst out, but Carl's voice overrode hers.

'Don't try to get away from the point, Rachel. What were you doing in Paris? Why did you go there?'

'Oh, I had my reasons.' Her voice was faintly mocking now, and a smile curved her mouth.

'If it wasn't work, then——' Lisa stopped short.

She could only think of one other reason why Rachel would desert the man she was to marry.

'Another man?' Rachel finished the sentence for her smoothly. 'Wouldn't you like to know—both of you?'

'To be quite honest,' Carl's voice had a note of chilly finality, 'I couldn't care less!'

Then he turned and swept out, slamming the door as he went.

'Well, that's that,' said Rachel after a moment, her voice light and unconcerned.

'Rachel, you can't just let him go like that!' Lisa protested.

'Of course I can. He'll come back tomorrow—or the next day.'

'I don't think so.'

'Of course he will!' Rachel's voice sharpened. 'Honestly, darling, you're so naïve when it comes to men. He loves me, he'll come back. If nothing else——' the smile touched her lips again. She looked like a predator. '—he's curious. He'll want to know why I went off to Paris. And now I'm going to bed. You can tell me all your news tomorrow.'

Yawning, stretching gracefully, she turned towards the hall. 'I've put your things in the spare bedroom, Mouse. You don't mind, do you?'

'Rachel—about Paris——' Lisa hesitated, unable to find the right words. Her sister turned and smiled over one white-clad shoulder.

'It rained, most of the time,' she said, and the bedroom door closed behind her with a firm click.

Lisa's clothes had been dropped on the spare room bed in an untidy heap. She put them away mechanically, then undressed and got into bed. For several hours, it seemed, she tossed and turned, the day reeling itself before her eyes like a film that had gone out of control. The sunny bay, the underwater world, the candlelit dinner table, Maria's furious face, the expression in Carl's eyes when he walked into the lounge and saw Rachel there.

And woven in and out of it all was the powerful memory of Carl's hands, his arms warm about her, his kisses incinerating her body.

How could Rachel walk out on a man like that? How could she torment him the way she had? Lisa knew the answer. Rachel could do these things because she could have any man she wanted. But Lisa couldn't. And Lisa, as she turned over in bed and tried to blot out the pictures her mind fed her, was only just beginning to realise that, against her better judgement and certainly against her own will, she wanted a man she couldn't possibly have, not ever.

It was another lovely sunny day when she woke early in the morning. The flat was silent when she left her room and the door to Rachel's room was closed.

The flagstones leading to the swimming pool were already warmed by the sun, and pleasant to her bare feet as she went for a swim. The pool had only one occupant—a middle-aged man who left shortly after Lisa arrived. She dived in from the deep end, welcoming the first shock of cool water. Then she swam strongly from end to end, refusing to allow herself to stop until her body cried out for rest. She turned on to her back and let the water hold her as she stared up at the pure blue sky.

She had hoped that the thoughts that had visited her before she slept were caused by exhaustion and reaction to Rachel's return. But they were still with her. She was strongly attracted to the man who was going to marry her sister. She had no doubt in her mind that Carl and Rachel would marry. If Rachel wanted it to happen, it would happen. And she wouldn't have come back to Minorca if she hadn't wanted Carl. There could be no other reason.

As for Lisa herself—she remembered that yesterday should have been his wedding day. It was natural that he would want to be with someone, anyone, instead of brooding alone. As for the scene in the bedroom—Lisa turned in the water and began to swim again, keeping her face beneath the surface and her eyes open, watching the white tiles slip by below—it had been brought about by his longing for Rachel. Only that. If it hadn't been Lisa, it would probably have been someone else.

She suddenly remembered Maria, small and lovely and still wanting Carl. If he had been alone when Maria had called, perhaps—Lisa pushed the thought from her mind and concentrated on being glad, for her sister's sake, that Carl hadn't been alone when his sister-in-law arrived.

By the time Mike arrived she had had a bath and shampooed her hair. At first, hearing the car engine slow and then stop below the patio where she sat, Lisa thought that Carl had returned. Her heart flipped crazily and she almost ran into her bedroom. Then Mike's tall, rangy figure appeared outside the gate.

'Hello, stranger——' he gave her a hug and a light friendly kiss, then kissed her again, more deeply, as she held on to him. 'Mmmm, I'm glad I dropped by,' he teased. 'And to think that all I was after was some breakfast! However, if there's something more tempting on the menu——'

'Have you seen Carl?' She wriggled out of his arms, to his obvious disappointment, and went into the kitchen, where the kettle was beginning to hiss.

Mike followed her, leaning on the door-frame. 'Not this morning. I'm sorry about having to leave you with him yesterday, love, but that engine had to take priority. We can't manage without it.'

'So you don't know that Rachel's back?'

He straightened, eyes blank with surprise for a moment.

'No—no, I didn't know that. When?'

'Late last night.'

'Has she seen Carl?'

'Oh yes. They had a row.'

Mike shrugged. 'That's their way of communicating. How do you feel about coming to Mercadel with me today? It's time you did a bit of sightseeing.'

'I don't know whether Rachel's planned anything or not.'

'Does that matter? I'm not inviting Rachel, I'm inviting you.' His grey eyes held hers, then he smiled, the warm smile that lit up his face. 'If Carl and Rachel are having one of their feuds, you'd be safer out of the range of fire, and you know it.'

Lisa returned the smile, and felt herself relaxing as he helped her to carry breakfast to the patio. Mike was so normal, so reliable. Mike was—safe, quite unlike Carl, she thought gratefully.

'There's a church on the hill way above Mercadel,' he explained as he buttered a slice of toast. 'It's called Our Lady of El Toro. Well worth seeing, and the view from the roof's——'

Then he stopped, his eyes fixed on the doorway. Turning, Lisa saw that Rachel was standing there.

CHAPTER EIGHT

RACHEL was still wearing the white lace-trimmed negligee and as she stepped on to the patio she pulled a white ribbon from her hair, shaking her head so that her long tresses swirled and settled over her shoulders. Her hair gleamed like copper in the sun.

'Oh, I thought you were Carl,' she said, her voice flat as she looked down at Mike.

'Sorry to disappoint you. So you came back after all.'

'I said I would!' she snapped back at him. Lisa was aware of sudden tension in the air, as real as a cloud blotting out the sun.

'Be a darling, Mouse, and get some coffee, will you?' Rachel sank on to a chair in a drift of fragrant white.

'I had wondered,' Lisa heard Mike say as she went obediently to the kitchen for another cup and saucer, 'if this time you would just keep on going.'

'I wanted to come back. To Carl. He loves me—remember?'

'If you say so,' Mike drawled with studied insolence as Lisa began to pour out Rachel's coffee.

'The poor darling's a bit ruffled just now, of course——' Rachel shot a look at Lisa from beneath thick black lashes, obviously wondering how much Mike had been told. 'But he'll come round.'

Mike finished his coffee, put the cup down, and got to his feet. He leaned back against the patio wall, hands resting on the top. His brown arms gleamed in the sunlight. 'You know, Rachel, it would serve you right if he turned you down.'

'But he won't.'

'If I were him, I'd decorate a wall with you.' A steely note crept into his even voice.

Rachel looked up at him. 'And you'd enjoy every minute of it, wouldn't you, darling?' she said sweetly. 'But luckily for me, it's none of your business. Just because you're Carl's business partner, you think that gives you the right to interfere with his personal life?'

Mike's eyes narrowed, went cold. 'I wouldn't touch his—personal life with a barge-pole!'

'I know you wouldn't!' Rachel's voice was suddenly ragged, ugly. Lisa was baffled by the sheer antagonism that leapt across the warm, soft air between them.

'Talking of the business——' she interrupted before the quarrel developed any further, 'I want to book a trip by boat some time, Mike.'

He held Rachel's gaze for a few seconds longer before turning to Lisa. All the warmth was back in his face, as though nothing had happened to chase it in the first place. 'Any time you like. What about the day after tomorrow? I haven't got any bookings at all, so we could take the boat to a nice little bay that I know. I'll bring some food, and we can swim and sunbathe.'

'Why don't we all go?' Rachel's cool voice asked unexpectedly.

'You—on a boat? It isn't a luxury liner,' Mike said crushingly. 'Strictly for the peasants, like me and Lisa.'

Rachel ignored him. 'All four of us.'

He scowled at her. A lesser mortal would have realised that he didn't welcome the suggestion, but Rachel simply fluttered her eyelashes at him and added, 'It would be fun—wouldn't it, Lisa?'

'Would Carl want to go?' Lisa asked doubtfully.

'Of course, if I want him to. The day after tomorrow, then.' Rachel poured out more coffee. Mike straightened, pushing himself up from the wall.

'I can hardly wait,' he said bleakly. 'Look, Lisa, I've got to go down to the harbour for a few minutes. I'll be back to collect you in ten minutes. Does that give you enough time to get ready?'

'Plenty.'

'Good. Bring a swimsuit.'

'Where are you going?' Rachel wanted to know.

Mike stopped at the top of the stairs. 'I'm taking Lisa to Mercadel for lunch. We're going to have a look at El Toro. And you're not invited, Rachel,' he added firmly. 'Strictly for me and my girl.'

Her mouth tightened. She had pushed a dark green cushion beneath her head and it made a perfect background for her lovely hair and face. 'I wanted you to come shopping with me, Mouse!'

'Another day,' Mike's voice took on its undertone of iron again. 'Today, she's all mine. Ten minutes, Lisa.'

'He's impossible!' Rachel stormed as he went downstairs. 'I don't know what's wrong with the man! To tell you the truth, Mouse, I'm not sure that I should approve of you going out with him.'

'You asked him to look after me while I was here,' Lisa reminded her tartly. She didn't know why Lisa and Mike disliked each other so much, but it was their concern, not hers. She liked Mike a lot and she didn't want to have to take sides in Rachel's quarrels.

'I didn't realise then how impossible he could be!' Rachel's voice was sulky. Clearly she would have preferred Lisa to change her plans and go shopping. Lisa's mouth set in a firm line and she went to get ready.

She put on a sleeveless dress in primrose yellow with a round neckline and fitted waist, tying her hair back loosely with a yellow scarf. Over one arm she draped a cream shawl in case the temperature dropped.

'Lisa?' Rachel called from the patio. 'Darling, have you got a nail-file handy?'

'My bag's on the divan—help yourself.' It was not Rachel's habit to go and get things for herself. Easier to call for help than to walk to her own room for a nail-file. Lisa smiled at her reflection in the mirror, picked up a swimsuit and towel, and went into the lounge.

Rachel was sitting on the divan, Lisa's open bag by her side, the nail-file lying in her lap. The sheaf of photographs Lisa had pushed into her bag and forgotten were in Rachel's hands, and she was leafing slowly through them.

'Mouse, where on earth did you get these?'

A stab of alarm ran through Lisa at the strange note in her sister's voice. She reached out for the photographs, but Rachel held on to them, studying each one.

'They're just photographs that Carl took.'

'When?'

Lisa moistened her lips. 'Yesterday, at the villa.'

'Carl took you to the villa?' Rachel looked up at her, the green eyes carefully blank. 'You didn't tell me about that, Mouse. Come to think of it,' she added slowly, 'you didn't tell me why he was with you last night when you got back here so late.'

Lisa explained as briefly as she could about the skin-diving lesson, the broken engine, and Carl's part in it all. She realised, watching her sister's politely interested expression, that she was probably explaining it badly.

'And the photographs?' Rachel prompted silkily when she had finished.

'Carl just decided to take them—I don't know why.'

'But they're very good.' Rachel's long slim fingers continued to riffle through them. 'You're—you look lovely in them, darling. I must admit that I had no idea how beautiful you are.'

Lisa's laugh was shaky. 'I thought that I looked terrible—my hair out of its usual style, and no make-up on. Carl's a good photographer, that's all.' She remembered his voice saying, 'I only take the pictures. I don't create the beauty. It has to be there—waiting to be warmed into life.'

The memory of Carl's lips warming her into life brought a glow to her face just as Rachel, still studying the pictures, said slowly, 'You look—different. As though something wonderful had just happened to you.' Then her head lifted and she studied Lisa through half-closed eyes. 'I wonder what it could have been, Mouse?'

'I told you—a good photographer can make the camera lie.'

'He is good, isn't he?' Rachel agreed at last. She smiled, her eyes suddenly as clear as green rock pools. 'And he likes to work all the time—on any subject he can find.' She tapped the pictures thoughtfully against her knee for a moment before finally handing them over. 'How lucky for you that you were there at the right time, Mouse. Now you've really got something special to remind you of this holiday, haven't you?'

The strange note was there again, and the eyes were slightly thoughtful as they rested on Lisa's face. The photographs seemed to scorch her fingers. She looked for one last, fleeting moment on the lovely wide-eyed face in the top photograph, then deliberately tore the pieces of board across.

'They're not really me.' She smiled a stiff smile

at her sister. She could hear footsteps on the stairs, the creak of the gate opening, and was filled with gratitude for Mike, who was coming back to rescue her.

'It would be silly of me to keep them,' she was saying when the door was pushed open and Carl walked into the lounge.

His dark eyes took in Lisa, standing in the middle of the room, moving from her eyes to the torn photographs in her hand. Fury leapt into his gaze as it swept back to her face, then Rachel was on her feet and moving towards him.

'Darling!' She wound her arm through his and turned to smile at Lisa. 'Talk of the devil—I was just admiring those wonderful photographs you took yesterday, at the villa.'

'But your sister doesn't share your enthusiasm, I see,' he said icily, his challenging gaze boring through Lisa.

'They're not really me. I'd—I'd feel uncomfortable with them.' She tried to smile, to shrug with Rachel's grace, and failed miserably. 'I told you, Carl, I'm not a model, I'm just—ordinary.'

'Perhaps you're right.' Each word hit her like a poison-tipped dart. He held out his free hand and she put the torn photographs into it wordlessly. He opened his fingers and let the glossy pieces of paper slip, fragment by fragment, into the wastepaper basket.

'I came to collect my jacket,' he said coldly.

'You couldn't have arrived at a better time, darling,' Rachel told him, and Lisa looked at her sharply, wondering just what her sister meant.

But Rachel's eyes were innocent as she looked up at Carl. 'Why don't you take me somewhere very romantic and very expensive for lunch, and we'll have a long talk. Mike's taking Lisa to Mercadel, and I'll be alone if you don't take pity on me.'

For a moment it looked as though Carl was going to refuse, then he shrugged. 'Yes, if you like—you've got a few things to explain, after all.'

'Good! I won't be a moment——' She kissed him, then disappeared into her room with a whisk of fragrant white lace.

'And you and I have things to talk about too,' Carl turned to Lisa.

'I don't think so.' She picked up her bag and went on to the patio, crushing swimsuit and towel into the bag as she went. He followed her.

'About last night——'

'Don't worry. I told Rachel that you took pity on me and gave me dinner at the villa. As long as Maria keeps her mouth shut you're safe.'

'Safe?' His eyebrows rose, then fleeting irritation crossed his face. 'You really think that I care about what Rachel thinks?' He reached out, put his hand on her arm. Her skin tingled as though a mild electric shock had just run along it, and she pulled away.

'I have to hurry—I'm meeting Mike.'

'Lisa——!' But she kept going, down the stairs and out into the hot dusty road, past his red car and on towards the junction with the main road.

Mike arrived just as she reached the junction. He leaned over to open the passenger door and grinned at her as she got in. 'That's what I like to

see in my women—impatience to be with me
again,' he told her, sliding the car smoothly back
into the stream of traffic.

The church of El Toro stood high above
Mercadel, its entrance dominated by a huge
figure of Christ on the cross. Bushes and flowers
provided visual relief in the courtyard from the
dazzling, soaring white walls, and the great
church itself was cool and dim, its huge gilded
altar rising above them in the gloom. When Lisa
had studied the tapestries, the pews, the intricate
work of screens and windows Mike led her
outside again, and up a narrow staircase that led
to the roof. From a distance Lisa had thought
that the vast dome looked as though it had been
woven from brown material. Now, as she stepped
on to the roof, she realised that the dome was
covered by the same shiny brown tiles that roofed
many of the island's houses.

'I thought you might like to see the view.
Watch it—if you fall over there's a long drop.
The perfect excuse to get my arms round you!'
Mike grinned. When they reached the bordering
wall she was quite glad of his strength beside her,
and his powerful arm encircling her. It was like
looking down from a plane. The hill the church
was built on dropped sharply away to the floor of
a valley far below. The houses were so small that
Lisa felt she could pick them up between thumb
and forefinger. Tiny cars crawled along thread-
like roads and the fields were a carpet of green,
white, grey and brown, with the blue sea making
a misty border in the distance.

'Come on——' Mike's arm tightened about her and he turned her away from the view eventually, 'I'm starving! Let's eat.'

'Do you think Rachel and Carl will get married?' Lisa asked during the meal.

'Probably.'

'So you really do think they love each other?'

He stared, then laughed. 'What has that to do with it? I said they'd probably get married, I didn't say anything about love.'

'It's the same thing.'

'Not as far as your sister and Carl are concerned.' She gaped at him, confused, and he grinned. 'Think it out, Lisa. Has Rachel ever really loved anyone? Totally, to the exclusion of everything else? As soon as a good job turned up in Paris, remember, she left Carl in the lurch. That's not love.'

'There wasn't a modelling session in Paris,' Lisa suddenly remembered.

'How do you know?' he asked quickly.

'Carl told us last night. And Rachel didn't deny it.'

'So he found her out? It was inevitable, I suppose. She should have realised that he knows everyone in the trade. He could easily check up on her.'

'Did you know?'

'I guessed. I've known your sister for a long time—longer than Carl. I know her little ways.'

'Do you think she went to Paris to meet a man?'

Mike stared down at his plate. 'With Rachel, anything's possible.'

'But she came back here, to Carl. She still wants to marry him.'

'So he must be the best bargain she's got where marriage is concerned,' he said indifferently.

'You make her sound like—like a praying mantis!'

'Do I? Look, Lisa, I know Rachel's your sister, but I also know that she's shallow, self-absorbed, and not inclined to look on life as anything other than an ongoing party.'

'And Carl?'

'I like him, you know that. He's real, in an unreal profession. But on the other hand, he's only a man. Rachel's well-known, undeniably beautiful, and very sweet when she wants to be. Carl's flattered by her attention and her interest. They're two beautiful people—they belong together like salt and pepper, or elegant book-ends. She made a play for him as soon as they met and he fell for it hook, line and sinker.'

'How can you be sure of that?' Lisa hated the picture he was painting for her, the insincerity and the fragility of it all.

'I was there. I introduced them. My darling Lisa, it all began in front of my very eyes.'

'But if it's as temporary as you think they might not marry each other.'

'True. If they realise the dangers in time.'

'And if they go ahead?'

'They'll have a marvellous time for three months—maybe even six,' he said thoughtfully. 'Then the bubble will burst.'

'Haven't you thought of warning them?'

'They're both adults. Nobody can tell Rachel what to do, you of all people must know that. As for Carl—he's been around. He's hardly a novice when it comes to women. Let him make his own mistakes. Who knows, it might even work out.'

'But you don't think so,' Lisa said slowly.

'What does it matter what I think?' Mike's voice was suddenly impatient. 'What does it matter what happens? Let them go ahead and have their wedding. The bridesmaid and the best man have their own lives to live, right? And before you think up one more question, I'd better warn you that I'm not interested in Rachel or Carl. This is our day!'

They drove to Son Bou, where the breakers crashed on to wide white sands, scattering their lacy aftermath far up the shallow beach. They swam, then visited a restaurant with a small dance floor. It was late by the time they drove back to the flat. About a mile out of the village Mike stopped the car.

'This is my favourite view at night. Come and have a look at it.'

They were at the side of the road leading down into the village. The ground fell away in a gentle slope. Below and before them the moon cut a straight broad path across the sea, a bridge from the village to the horizon. Slightly to their right the harbour lay like a jewelled brooch, outlined by the lamps all around it. Here and there green fronds from the palm trees were caught in the light like fragments of velvet. Some of the boats in the harbour were lit, and the restaurants and houses along the street threw their own light on to the still dark water within the stone walls. Above, the sky was studded with stars. The moon, the sky's centrepiece, put the finishing touch to the fairy-tale scene.

The shawl slipped from Lisa's shoulders and Mike settled it back in place, his fingers brushing her neck with a gentle pressure. When he retained his hold, turned her to face him, it seemed only natural to move into his arms and lift her face for his kiss.

His lips were strong and yet tender. It was a kiss that asked for her response without demanding it, as Carl's kisses had demanded. She was able to welcome his gentleness without guilt, and time seemed to stand still as she remained locked in his arms, returning his kisses, holding him close.

When they finally got back into the car they drove the rest of the way without speaking. Mike cut the engine at the top of the slight hill from the junction and they coasted silently to the door. He leaned across and kissed her, then got out and opened the passenger door, gathering her out of the car and into his arms in one smooth movement. When he released her she smiled up at him, then her gaze went above his head, attracted by a slight movement. Someone—Rachel, she was sure—was leaning over the patio wall. By the time Mike turned to look the figure had gone.

'What is it?' he asked.

'Nothing. I just thought I saw—a bird, or something.'

'More likely to be a bat at this time of night.' He kissed her nose. 'Tomorrow I have an all-day fishing trip. Come with me.'

'I'd be bored.'

He sighed. 'Is there no romance in your soul? Okay, I'll see you the day after. In the meantime, don't fall for any handsome dark-eyed islanders—promise?'

Lisa laughed up at him. 'I promise.'

'Good.' He kissed her again, a lingering kiss that left them both breathless, then released her reluctantly. 'Sleep well—and thanks for being you.'

There was no sign of Rachel when Lisa went into the apartment, though she was certain that she could sense a delicate trace of perfume on the patio, as though Rachel had been sitting there when Mike's car stopped.

Rachel's bedroom door was closed and Lisa hesitated before it, then turned away and went to her own room. She had no way of knowing how her sister's day with Carl had turned out. Best to leave her alone until the morning.

CHAPTER NINE

IT seemed to Lisa on the following afternoon that she and Rachel had visited every dress shop in Mahon, the island's main town. Rachel was at her happiest when she was buying clothes, and all her sulkiness and suspicion vanished as she turned each purchase into an impromptu fashion show for the other shoppers.

She had said nothing about the previous day, apart from asking Lisa if she had enjoyed herself.

'Don't you find Mike boring?' she asked silkily, and when Lisa indignantly started to protest, her sister held up one elegant hand to stop her.

'You don't have to jump to his defence so quickly, Mouse.' Her voice was cool and patronising. 'All right, perhaps you might find him interesting—after all, you haven't known many interesting men, have you? But he's so—so stolid, so set in his ways.'

'Just because he likes to think for himself?'

'Is that what you call it?' Rachel drawled, and Lisa subsided, fuming inwardly but aware that she and Rachel could argue all day and Rachel still wouldn't change her views.

'Let's buy something really nice for you, darling,' Rachel decided suddenly.

'I've got all the clothes I need.'

'Mouse, no woman ever has all the clothes she

needs!' Rachel was shocked at the idea. 'Besides, I want to buy you something. You can wear it at the wedding.'

'You've fixed a new date?'

'What? Oh—not exactly——' Rachel said vaguely, her long fingers already riffling through a rack of dresses. 'But we will. What about this?'

The dress was soft and filmy, in shades of turquoise and green. It was beautiful—and it brought back a sudden painful memory of a sun-splashed terrace, cool waxy white flowers against dark green leaves, Carl's fingers pushing the dress strap from her shoulder, his lips on hers——

'No!' Lisa said sharply, then added, confused, 'I-I don't think the colour's right for me.'

'But it's the same colour as the dress you wore in Carl's photographs, isn't it?' Rachel's voice was sweet, her eyes slightly narrowed.

'I don't really like that colour.'

Rachel shrugged, and returned the dress to the rack without further comment. 'What about this?'

The silk dress was cream-coloured, with draped bodice and sleeves, a flared skirt, and a demure lacy inset at the low neck. When Lisa tried it on the mirror showed how well the colour suited her newly acquired golden tan. Her chestnut brown hair curled softly just above her shoulders, and the material felt just right against her skin. It was perfect for her. They bought elegant high-heeled sandals to match, then Rachel suddenly announced that she was bored with shopping.

'Let's drive back slowly, drop all this stuff at the flat, then go out to dinner, just the two of us,' she suggested as they got into the hired car. She drove well, with the accomplished, flamboyant flourish she brought to everything she did.

They took the scenic coast road, stopping off for a leisurely drink. Evening had settled over the island by the time they approached the coast where the village lay. A few miles before they got there the car began to weave back and forth across the empty road.

Efficiently, without getting flustered, Rachel managed to steer the vehicle into the side of the road and stopped it. They got out and examined the flat tyre.

'Damn!' Rachel kicked it, then looked around at the deserted countryside, pushing her hair back from her face. 'Well, darling, now's your chance to demonstrate your skill at hitch-hiking.'

They didn't have long to wait. The first car to arrive stopped as soon as the middle-aged driver saw Rachel's elegant figure, in cream trouser suit with a long green scarf floating from her throat, leaning casually against the wing of the car. She spoke to him briefly, then packed Lisa and the shopping into the back seat of his large and comfortable vehicle, getting into the passenger seat in front herself.

'Our Good Samaritan's passing quite near Carl's villa, so we'll go there,' she threw the words over her shoulder. 'He can take us home.' Then she devoted her attention to their rescuer, charming him utterly. As Mike had said, every man fell for Rachel. Every man except Mike, Lisa realised—which was probably why her sister couldn't stand him.

Carl's scarlet sports car and a large sleek midnight blue saloon were parked together on the wide sweep of gravel before the villa.

'Good—he's home.' Rachel leaned forward and hit the horn imperiously before getting out of the car. As Lisa disentangled herself from boxes and parcels and stepped on to the gravel, Carl appeared on the balcony above.

'We're marooned!' Rachel called to him, her lovely face uplifted in the dimming evening light. 'Come and rescue us!'

He started down the steps towards her as Lisa went across the gravel and round behind the scarlet car. The staircase's graceful curved lines provided the perfect setting for him, dressed as he was in a dark blue velvet jacket, beautifully cut trousers that emphasised his long legs, and a frilled shirt as crisp and white as fresh snow. She had never seen him looking so handsome. His black hair was well-groomed and his lean brown face was aristocratic above the formal wear.

He even moved in a different way—still with the suppleness of a panther, but combining it with a controlled grace that gave him maturity.

He was suddenly the sort of man she had imagined Rachel would marry—extremely good-looking, successful, mature. He belonged, now, with the big white villa and the powerful scarlet car Lisa stood beside. Mike had said that Carl and Rachel were two beautiful people. He had

said it disparagingly, but all at once Lisa realised
that he had spoken the truth. This new,
devastating Carl was part of Rachel's world. A
world that Lisa could never hope to enter.

Ironically, it was at that moment, just as she
recognised the gulf between them, that she knew
that she was deeply in love with her sister's
future husband.

If her emotions showed in her face, Carl didn't
seem to notice as he flicked a casual glance at her.
Then he reached the bottom of the steps, and his
attention was focussed on Rachel, who was
waiting for him with outstretched hands. It was
only when Carl and Rachel met, joining hands,
that Lisa took her eyes from them and noticed the
man who came downstairs behind Carl. He too
was in evening dress and he too was darkly
handsome, though older and heavier than Carl.

'Rachel? I didn't expect to see you here. And
Lisa——' Carl nodded in Lisa's direction, but
kept his dark eyes fixed on Rachel's face as she
poured out her story.

'But of course you were right to come here!'
The other man broke in before Carl could speak.
The admiration in his gaze was quite unmistakable, and Rachel glowed at him. 'What an
unfortunate experience! I will see to it that you
get back home safely. I can only regret that we
had to meet in these circumstances,' he said
warmly, in heavily-accented, stiff English.
'Carlos——?'

Carl made the introductions, then turned to the
rescuer, talking to him in Spanish. As the older

man bowed over Rachel's hand, then her own, Lisa could only stare at Carl, his words echoing in her mind.

'My brother Eduardo——'

If Eduardo was at the villa, then probably his wife was with him. And now nothing could stop a meeting between Rachel and Maria. As though he could hear her thoughts, Carl looked at her briefly, raised his eyebrows and shrugged faintly. Obviously he felt that the next few hours were in the lap of the gods, she thought as she watched him transfer the shopping to the back seat of his own car.

'Are we interrupting a dinner-party?' Rachel asked as the four of them went up the staircase after waving goodbye to their rescuer. Her hand rested lightly, possessively, on Carl's arm.

'A business dinner. My brother, his wife, and the family lawyer.'

So Maria was at the villa. Lisa, walking behind her sister and Carl, felt her heart contract.

'But the business is almost over,' Eduardo assured them, as they went into the house. The dining-room was lit, as it had been on Lisa's former visit, by candles. This time two elaborate branched silver candlesticks were in use so that the entire table and a good part of the room could be seen. The meal was over, and the table held coffee cups, liqueur glasses, and balloon glasses for brandy.

Maria, in an eye-catching dress of flame-coloured silk, stood by the window. Her shining black hair was piled on top of her head, her rounded body was displayed to advantage by the clever cut of the dress, and diamonds glittered at her throat, in her small, well-formed ears, and on her fingers and wrists.

Her eyes fastened on Lisa immediately, the hard flat glitter creeping into her gaze. When her husband introduced her to Rachel, shock made her face go completely blank for a few seconds, then she recovered herself.

'I-I can't think why Carlos didn't invite you to dine with us tonight,' she purred. 'And, of course, your—sister.' There was a very faint pause between the last few words, but Carl said easily.

'I didn't think that a business dinner was the right occasion, Maria.'

'It almost seems as though Carlos has been reluctant to let us meet,' Maria said maliciously. 'I wonder why?'

As the stocky elderly lawyer was introduced Lisa watched the Spanish woman, and saw her eyes moving constantly between herself, Rachel and Carl. Obviously Maria was trying to work out why she had met the wrong woman in Carl's villa the other night. But it was equally obvious that Carl was right when he said that Maria's visit had been secret, and her objections to his marriage made for personal reasons. Eduardo made it very clear that any marriage that brought Rachel into his family was acceptable.

Carl, calling for Francisca and ordering food for his unexpected guests, seemed to be quite at ease, unaware of the dangers of the situation.

As Rachel and Lisa ate the meal put before them Maria ordered Francisca around, fussed over their comfort, and behaved as though she was the hostess. Rachel retaliated by staying close to Carl, touching him often, smiling intimately into his eyes, showing Maria that Carl was her property.

Lisa found it hard to believe that the men weren't aware of the hostility between those two beautiful, possessive women. Eduardo and the lawyer kept the conversation circulating smoothly, and Carl, at the head of the table, seemed to be quite relaxed.

While extra places were being set he had pushed one of the candlesticks away so that the head of the table was shadowy, and had eased his chair back slightly. From where Lisa sat she could only see one velvet-clad arm, a snowy cuff with gold links, a strong brown hand shaping itself round the voluptuous curve of a brandy glass. Now and then she glimpsed the sparkle of his dark eyes watching them all, though he had little to say.

Maria's chance to cause trouble came after Rachel and Lisa had finished eating. Francisca brought fresh coffee, and disappeared—on her way home, Lisa realised, and didn't look at the shadows where Carl sat. The men took their coffee and went to the study to continue their business discussion, and the three women were left alone.

'And when do you and Carlos plan to marry?' Maria asked sweetly.

'We haven't arranged a date yet,' Rachel's voice was also honeyed.

'You must invite Eduardo and myself to attend.' Maria gave a tinkling laugh. 'A wedding is a happy occasion, and happiness should be shared. A family should have no secrets. Should it, Lisa?'

Lisa was forced to look up. The mocking gleam had returned, and Maria was looking directly at her, challenging her. If she had been more sophisticated, more worldly, Lisa might have found the words to stop Maria's malice in its tracks. But she could only sit helplessly and wait. Eduardo wasn't there. Maria could show her hand a little—enough—without getting into trouble herself.

'And since we are to become part of the same family, we must all be friends, the three of us,' the lilting voice went on. 'I'm sure we will be, though this is only our first meeting, Rachel. And——' a pause, then she went on, 'our second meeting, Lisa.'

Rachel took the bait at once. 'I didn't know you'd met my sister?'

Maria put a beringed hand to her mouth. 'Have I said something wrong?'

'I told you that I had dinner here the other night——' Lisa said swiftly. 'Maria happened to arrive while I was here. We met briefly.'

'And I very foolishly thought that she was Carlos's fiancée,' Maria's voice was smooth.

A faint frown knotted Rachel's brows.

'Why on earth should you think that?'

'It was an easy mistake to make,' the Spanish woman prattled on, her voice soaring and dipping round the table like bird in flight. 'An Englishwoman, alone with Carlos late at night—and when I saw your sister coming from the bedroom I naturally thought that she——'

The door opened and Eduardo breezed in, followed by the lawyer and Carl.

'Maria, time to take Señor Cavero back to Mahon,' Eduardo said cheerfully, without a pause. Maria rose at once, kissed Carl and thanked him for the meal. She was a relaxed woman who had enjoyed an evening with friends—nothing more. The claws had been sheathed the moment the door opened, the malice in her eyes swept away at once.

'But Rachel and Lisa haven't finished their coffee yet,' she protested. 'We must wait until they're ready to travel with us.'

Rachel rested her elbows on the table, entwined her fingers, and smiled up at Maria. 'Please don't worry about us. Carl can drive us back later, can't you, darling?'

'Of course.' Lisa saw his gaze travel between Rachel to Maria, then it stopped, unexpectedly, on her. She stared down at the polished table, unable to meet his eyes. She wanted to get out of the villa, to escape from the smouldering anger that was probably building up behind Rachel's smiling face. But there was no escape. She was trapped.

It seemed a long time before the others left, but finally they went out of the dining-room, Carl going with them to their car.

Rachel waited until the voices had died away to a murmur from below before she broke the silence.

'What a bitch that woman is! Obviously she's madly jealous over Carl.' She got up, moved to the window, turned. 'And how unlucky you were, darling, to be caught by her the other night—all alone with my fiancé.'

Lisa felt colour flood into her face. 'Rachel, surely you don't believe her!'

'Of course not. How could I think such terrible things of my sister—my loyal, loving sister!' Rachel's temper was magnificent and frightening when it surfaced. Even in the room's shadows her eyes flashed green fire and her tawny mane glowed about her face.

'What is there to believe?' she swept on before Lisa could say anything. 'Alone together in this house, late at night—and Maria saw you coming from the bedroom. If you'd seen your face when she let that little pearl of information drop, Mouse! You were never able to deceive me—never. I could always tell when you were lying, couldn't I? And now you want me to believe that you were only paying my fiancé a friendly, sisterly call? Come on, darling,' her voice grew hard, 'I'd have to be a complete idiot to believe that!'

CHAPTER TEN

'AT least let me explain!' Lisa jumped up and faced her sister across the table.

'Explain? Explain what? You just thought you'd have some fun with my fiancé while I was safely out of the way—and you got caught. Be honest about it!'

'Rachel, please listen——'

'All right, I'll listen. Tell me about it,' Rachel invited, gripping the back of a chair so tightly that her knuckles gleamed white in the candle-light. 'Tell me that it was all innocent. Tell me that Maria didn't interrupt anything!'

'That's what I'm——' Lisa stopped, and Rachel's eyes widened, then turned to ice. Lisa was recalling those brief moments in the dark bedroom, Carl lifting her and carrying her to the bed—his hands warm on her skin, his lips moving from her throat to her shoulder——

'Carl's a very handsome man,' Rachel went on, a tremor in her voice. 'A charming man. And, at that moment, a lonely man. How could you resist the temptation to console him, to enjoy a little stolen romance while my back was turned? Easy to forget that he was mine, wasn't it?' Her laughter had a chill, menacing ring to it. 'No wonder you looked so disappointed when you walked into the flat and discovered that I'd come back!'

Lisa had learned early in life to hold her tongue when Rachel flared up. It was best to let the storm rage until it had exhausted itself. But now she found anger rising in her own mind. She was tired of being used by Carl, by Maria and by Rachel to further their own plans. It was time they learned that she had feelings, too.

'Don't be such a fool!' she almost shouted at her sister, and Rachel's face went blank with shock. 'You know as well as I do that no man's ever looked twice at me after he's seen you! Do you think I haven't suffered again and again because of your beauty? Do you honestly believe that a man like Carl would give me a passing glance? I'm too dull, too ordinary for him. He only brought me here for dinner because I'm your sister and you'd deserted us both!'

'Do you expect me to believe that?' Rachel rallied, but Lisa swept on.

'You should have had the sense to realise that you can't walk out on someone like that and expect him to be waiting when you feel like coming back. You should be darned glad that it was me he took out, and not some woman who might have been a real threat to you!'

'The English turn everything into a scene in a play,' said Carl's deep, amused voice, and Lisa whirled round. He was leaning against the door frame, arms folded. He looked as though he had been there for some time.

'Don't be so—so condescending!' she blazed at him, and was horrified to hear her voice shake on the last word. She blinked hard

against the stinging sensation at the back of her
eyes.

'I gathered from Maria's smug look that she'd
been causing trouble.' He went to the sideboard,
and lifted a brandy decanter.

'And I gather that you've been amusing
yourself with my sister while I was away!'

'Brandy, Rachel? Lisa? No? Well, Lisa, have I
been amusing myself with you? Or have you been
amusing yourself with me? Has the Mouse been
playing while the—cat's away?'

'Stop trying to make things worse, Carl!' Lisa
snapped at him.

'Rachel seems to think that you've been
enticing me—tempting me. You've got to remember, Rachel, that she's not a little girl any
more,' he went on smoothly. 'Or haven't you
even realised that yet?'

Rachel's voice dripped venom. 'I do now!'

'Can't you see he's just using me to annoy you,
Rachel—the way he's been using me all along!'

A frown drew Carl's well-shaped eyebrows
together and the teasing note vanished from his
voice. 'Using you? You think that's what I've
been doing?'

'Of course! Why would you have wasted time
on me at all, if you hadn't wanted to make Rachel
jealous? I'm not as naïve as you both think—I'm
intelligent enough to know when someone's
making a fool out of me!'

Her voice shook dangerously on the last two
words and she had to turn away from the eyes,
one pair vivid green, the other pair dark, that

seemed to be staring right into her bruised heart. 'Why can't you just get married, you two, and make each other unhappy? And count me out!' She threw the words over her shoulder.

'A very touching scene, Mouse darling, but not really convincing enough!' Rachel said coldly.

'Why do you call her by that stupid name all the time?' Carl demanded irritably.

'What?' Rachel was taken off guard, bewildered. 'I've called her that since she was a baby——'

'I thought we'd just agreed that your baby sister has grown up. Why can't you call her Lisa, or—what is it? Melissa! Why can't you call her Melissa, for God's sake!'

'Would it please you if I did?'

'It wouldn't matter one bit. But it might help your sister to feel like a woman, and not your inferior!'

Rachel's gasp was audible. 'That's ridiculous! I've never treated Mo—Lisa as though she was my inferior!'

Lisa turned to face them again. Rachel's white face was dominated by her furious eyes, her hands were curled into fists by her sides. Carl was standing by the table, a brandy glass in his hand.

'My dear Rachel,' he said slowly, deliberately, 'you treat everyone as though they were your inferiors. Lisa, Mike—and me. It's time someone pointed out to you that a beautiful face and a beautiful body——' he let his gaze move over her with studied indifference, and Lisa saw her sister flinch, '—and a considerable capacity for arousing sexual desire in every man you meet doesn't make you anyone's superior. In fact, I would be inclined to say that you're anything but——'

Rachel moved fast, but Carl was faster. Lisa didn't even see him put the glass down on the table before he caught Rachel's wrists. Her clawed, long-nailed fingers were only inches away from his face as the two of them stood motionless, his dark head bent over her. They might, in the candlelight, have been lovers frozen in an embrace if it hadn't been for the rage that twisted Rachel's lovely face.

'I'm not a gentleman, my darling,' Carl said at last, cold steel in his voice. 'If you ever try that on me again I'll throw you into the pool out there and I'll hold you under!'

'Let me go!' she panted, struggling against his grip. 'Let—me—go!'

Her fury was frightening to see. Lisa stepped forward, but before she could intervene Carl opened his fingers. Rachel staggered and almost fell, then she stormed past him, out of the room.

'Go after her, Carl!'

'Leave her alone.' Carl sat down at the table and picked up his glass. 'There's nowhere for her to go.' His face was hidden from Lisa, but she could see that he was breathing deeply and quickly, as though trying to bring his feelings under control.

She ran into the hall and out on to the wide balcony at the front of the house. A car engine started up as she reached the top of the staircase.

'Rachel!'

Her sister didn't look up at her. Gravel sprayed as the wheels of Carl's sports car spun too fast, then gripped. The car shot forward, went into a tight turn, then made for the gates. Rachel's long hair whipped about her face and her green chiffon scarf streamed out like a banner in the wind created by the car's speed. The vehicle hurtled through the gates, narrowly missing one of the stone pillars, then the tyres screamed as Rachel dragged the steering wheel round viciously to line up the front wheels with the road.

The rear lights flicked on and swung crazily as the back of the car slewed across the road. Then the engine accelerated and the car took off, its powerful roar quickly fading into silence.

'I was wrong,' Carl said blandly when Lisa went back to the dining-room. 'I must have forgotten to take the ignition key out.'

'She might kill herself!'

'Not Rachel. She's a good driver and she's got a highly-developed sense of survival. She won't kill herself. She might,' he added thoughtfully, 'damage my car. If she does she'll end up wishing she had killed herself.'

'Don't you care?' Lisa stood over him, her nails digging into the palms of her hands. She was aware that she was shaking, that there were tears in her eyes, tears of rage. She had watched her sister being humiliated and destroyed by this man who sat sipping fine old brandy as though he hadn't a care in the world.

He raised his eyebrows. 'Care?'

'About Rachel. How could you do that to her?'

'I had to take her attention away from you, didn't I? And I succeeded. She was so involved on the attack on her own character that she completely forgot what Maria had told her.'

Lisa gasped. 'You deliberately hurt her?'

'Little sister, Rachel isn't breakable. She has too high an opinion of herself to let anything that I say bother her.'

'I hope you're right.' Lisa recalled Rachel's white face, the violent way she had jerked the wheel round as she drove out on to the road. She had a feeling that Carl's jibes had gone deep, well below the cushion of self-esteem that protected Rachel most of the time.

'Of course I'm right.' He went to the sideboard, came back with a clean glass, and poured brandy into it. 'Drink this.'

'I hate the stuff!'

'Drink it!' His voice was suddenly a whiplash. 'I don't care whether you like it or not, you need it.' He touched her cheek lightly with the back of his hand. 'You're as cold as ice and you're trembling. You shouldn't let Maria upset you so much. She'd cause trouble at the gates of Heaven—if anyone was ever misguided enough to let her get there!'

Lisa sank into a chair. The brandy stung her throat, making her cough, but as she obediently sipped it a glow began to spread throughout her body, steadying her. 'I'm not used to scenes. Not like you and Rachel.'

'You won't believe it, of course, but I don't

like scenes either. I enjoy a quiet life. Your sister seems to have the ability to bring out my worst side.' Carl sat down at the table.

'It must be her considerable capacity for arousing sexual desire,' Lisa said tartly, and he stared at her for an astonished moment before throwing his head back and breaking into a roar of laughter. There was something infectious about the genuine peals of mirth, and a reluctant smile touched Lisa's lips.

'You know,' he said when he managed to stop laughing, 'Rachel doesn't make me laugh the way you do. I hadn't realised that before you arrived. Perhaps you're right—it's her sex appeal. Not a problem that you suffer from—and I'm only saying that before you do,' he added hurriedly. 'What was it again? Dull? Ordinary? I'm beginning to wonder if there's any point in telling you that you're quite wrong about yourself. Why did you tear up the photographs I took?'

The unexpected question took her by surprise. 'Rachel found them. They—I think they bothered her.'

'I can see that they would. But why throw them away for her sake? They were a gift from me to you—nothing to do with Rachel.' A hard note crept into his voice.

'I-I thought it was best.' Lisa couldn't meet his steady gaze. After a moment he said lightly, 'As it happens, I have my own set, little sister. And the negatives. So you haven't been able to wipe out that day after all.'

There was silence, then he set his empty

glass down on the table with a small, sharp sound.

'Now—what shall we do?' he asked.

'Have you got another car here?'

He shook his head.

'What about the beach buggy?'

'Mike has it. We could always have a good long talk. As a matter of fact, I did want to talk to you about something. When you were here the other night——'

'I'll have to get a taxi back to the flat,' Lisa interrupted. She had no desire to talk about the night Rachel had arrived back. 'Where's the telephone?'

'In the study, directly across the hall. There's an extension in my bedroom upstairs, if you'd like to use that,' he drawled, his eyes sparkling at her from beneath half-closed lids.

'Do you have a number I could call?'

'On the front cover of the pad by the phone. But there's no hurry, is there? Why don't you sit down again, have some more brandy? I'm sure we could think of a better alternative, if we put our heads together.'

'It's getting very late. May I use your phone?' she asked patiently.

Carl waved one hand in a casual, generous gesture. 'Feel free——' he said, and his accent gave added charm to the phrase.

The study was a small room with books lining two walls, big windows taking up the third, and the fourth covered with photographs, obviously taken by Carl. The phone was on the desk, and the number Lisa wanted was clearly indicated by the word 'taxis' printed beside it.

She picked up the receiver with a sense of relief and began to dial. Then a lean brown hand descended gently over her shoulder and landed on the receiver rest, depressing it. Another took the receiver from her fingers and replaced it. Carl's body held her captive against the desk at her back, she found when she spun round.

'I've just thought of a better alternative——' he said softly, looming over her.

CHAPTER ELEVEN

THERE was no way for Lisa to get past Carl without trying to push him out of the way. She stayed where she was, fighting down the tremor that had rippled through her body when his fingers touched hers.

'What—what are you talking about?' Her mouth was dry.

'Well——' the drawl was back, 'they've all gone away and marooned us here, together. And it seems to me that since Maria and Rachel already think the worst, is there any sense in fighting it, little sister? Why don't we just give in to fate—and make the most of our night here while we've got the opportunity?'

She felt the blood rush to her face, then drain away. 'You—you must be out of your mind!'

Although she couldn't let her eyes meet his she knew that he was looking her over slowly, and every nerve-end tingled under the touch of his dark eyes.

'You're not as bad as all that, little sister. And since you lost your temper with Rachel you've changed—matured—there's a glow about you that makes you very, very desirable——' his voice caressed her, low and suggestive and with an undercurrent of amusement that told her that he was, once again, deliberately embarrassing her.

'Carl, get out of my way!' She pushed against his hard chest with both hands, but he just trapped her fingers in his.

'What are you going to do—walk home?'

'If I have to!'

'I can't be as unattractive as all that, little sister. When you were speaking to Rachel earlier, you made me sound—pretty good.' His deep voice caressed her like velvet. 'Changed your mind already?'

She was keenly aware of the firm mouth only inches away from hers. She remembered the sweet thrill of his kisses, and was sure he must know that she was trembling.

'Lisa?' She wouldn't look at him, but when one hand held her chin, turning her face towards his, she knew, despairingly, that her longing for him must be blazing from her treacherous eyes. The teasing smile fled, his brows swiftly dipped into a slight frown, then she closed her eyes, unable to meet his gaze any longer.

'Lisa?' He said it again, this time softly, with a puzzled question in his voice. Then, at last, his lips were on hers, and the agony of waiting was over.

She tried with all her strength to stay passive, to let her mouth lie still beneath his, but it was impossible. She reached up to hold him, parted her lips beneath his, and gave herself up to his kiss. It was a joy that she had been hungering for all her life. It was the moment when she stepped, confidently, across the barrier that divided youth and maturity. When Carl raised his head, she opened her eyes and saw that the frown was still stitched between his dark brows.

'Whatever made me think that you were only Rachel's little sister?' he asked, his voice hoarse, and she thrust her fingers deep into his hair and pulled his mouth down to hers again. It wasn't the time to talk.

He teased her lips apart and a fire spread along her limbs, into her heart, consuming her brain, as she held him. When he finally released her mouth and let his kisses travel slowly over her neck and throat she slid her hands inside his jacket, caressing the muscular back that seemed to scorch her palms through his shirt.

His arms tightened about her, and still she wanted, desperately, to be closer to him, to be part of him. It was then, when her longing for him was about to engulf her completely, that she opened her eyes and found herself staring over his shoulder straight into her sister's face.

Lisa's hands stilled on Carl's back, and a shock ran through her body. From the blurred mass of photographs covering the opposite wall Rachel's had leapt into stark clarity. She was pictured from the back, and she was wearing a gold dress wrapped round her body sari-style. She was looking over her shoulder at the camera with a sulky mouth and a sultry gaze that, to Lisa, seemed to hold accusation.

She stiffened in Carl's arms. 'What's wrong?' He tried to kiss her, but she pushed him away, stepping back out of his arms, dragging her gaze with difficulty from the photograph.

'Lisa——?' He tried to catch at her hand, but she pulled away and made for the hall, her hands at her face.

'Carl, phone for a taxi—please! Just let me get out of here!'

He stood in the study doorway, his hair tousled by her fingers, his face dark with anger. The tenderness had gone. 'Up to your tricks again, little sister?' he asked icily. 'Just stringing me along, were you?'

'For heaven's sake, Carl, stop and think about what we're doing!'

'Think? Lisa, you have a strange way of looking at things. If men and women stopped to think every time they—every time they wanted to kiss,' he said hoarsely, 'the world would be a sad place!'

'You're going to marry my sister!'

'Who said I was going to marry your sister? I'm not sure about that any more. And don't try to make up my mind for me, Lisa—I don't allow anyone to do that!'

'Of course you'll marry her. You love her!' She made it a statement, not a question.

Colour deepened the tan over his high cheekbones. 'And don't make any decisions for me on that score either! Let's talk about you, shall we? You—and the way you can switch from ice to fire and back again without any warning. Or are you just a very good actress? Was I right when I said you could be amusing yourself with me?'

Lisa caught her breath. The accusation was like a slap in the face. 'I'm going back to the flat—now,' she kept her voice as even as she could.

'So there's to be no explanation.' Carl's face was suddenly bleak.

'Please phone for a taxi. I'll wait outside for it.' She turned towards the front door, praying that he would just do as she asked. But as she reached out for the door handle steel fingers caught her arm, swinging her round.

'I could take you right now, right here, if I wanted to,' Carl's voice was a sharp-edged weapon that seemed to slice the flesh from her bones. His fingers bit cruelly into her arm, reminding her of his strength and her own helplessness. 'I could teach you not to tease, little sister. And then, perhaps, I might be prepared to teach you what passion between a man and a woman can be like. What happens to ice when it meets an all-consuming fire. Oh——' he said huskily, '—I could teach you so much, Lisa. And we have all the time we need. We wouldn't be interrupted, would we?'

Fear welled up in her and she fought it back, refusing to let him see it. He was right; she was at his mercy. He could make her his prisoner throughout the long night and nobody would know.

She forced the panic down and made herself relax in order to ease the pain of his grip. Then she looked up into the dark, mocking eyes just above hers, made herself speak firmly, without a tremor in her voice.

'Yes, you could make me stay here. I'm not strong enough to fight you. If forcing me to make love with you against my will gives you pleasure, I'll have to submit.'

His lips parted, his eyes widened, blazing down into hers. For a moment she thought that her taunts had driven him too far—then he released her so abruptly that she almost fell.

'I'll take you home.' Each word was an icicle. Lisa rubbed her arm with shaking fingers, unable to believe that she had won. 'You haven't got a car.'

He threw the words over his shoulder as he began to ascend the stairs to the upper floor. 'No, but I've got a motor-bike.'

Lisa went into the dining-room, moving as though in a dream. She had shamed Carl into taking her back to the flat. She had defeated him in their battle of wills—but she knew he would never forgive her for drawing back from his embrace. She slopped some brandy into her glass and made herself drink it, glad to sit down for a moment. The candles were burning low and shadows gathered round the big table. She would never forget this room. Some of the most important moments of her life had been spent in it. The meal alone with Carl now seemed to her to be an oasis of happiness, distorted by Maria's jealousy, Rachel's fury. She got to her feet and put the empty glass down.

'You'll need——' Carl's mouth turned down at the corners when she spun round with a gasp. His eyes were like black stones as he surveyed her. 'Oh, don't worry, little sister, I'm not going to creep up behind you and throw you to the floor!' he jeered. 'Take these, you can't travel on the back of a bike in that.'

His gaze took in her simple lilac shift with as much appreciation as he would have bestowed on an oily rag. 'You can use the bedroom you used before. You're quite safe from my unbridled lust, but there's a key in the lock, just in case you want to make certain.'

There was indeed a key, but she didn't turn it. She knew only too well that Carl wouldn't touch her again. Not if she was the last woman on earth, she told herself bitterly.

He had given her a black polo-necked sweater and pale blue jeans. They were far too big for her and she had to fold the sweater sleeves back and roll up the legs of the jeans. Fortunately there was a belt which helped to anchor the jeans round her waist. The jersey smelled masculine and comforting, and she buried her nose in its warmth for a moment before she realised what she was doing.

Defiantly, ignoring the fact that from the neck down she looked like Charlie Chaplin, and the fact that Carl didn't care about her, she brushed her hair and put on some make-up and perfume. Then, slightly heartened, she went back to the dining-room.

Carl was standing by the window, staring out into the night. He had put on a bronze sweater and black cords, and his hair was uncombed and curly. He swung round when she spoke his name,

and laughter blazed unexpectedly into his eyes as
he took in the sweater and jeans. His mouth
twitched violently. It took him a moment to bring
his features under control, but when he finally
spoke his voice was hard. 'Shall we go?'

Outside Lisa waited while he opened the
carport and brought out the motor-bike. The air
was filled with scents from the garden, and
vibrant with the chirping of cicadas. The sky was
starry. It was hard to believe that such a perfect
night had been gathering outside the great white
house while so much drama was going on within
its walls.

'Just hold on tight and move with the bike on
the bends.' Carl threw one long leg over the
saddle and held out a hand to help her on to the
pillion. 'Ready?'

She put her arms about him. His sweater was
soft and warm beneath her fingers, and the palms
of her hands shaped themselves easily to the hard
strong muscles of his chest.

'Ready.'

She tried to look over his shoulder as they
roared along, but the wind whipped her hair
across her face, and strung tears to her eyes.
She soon gave up and tucked her face against
Carl's broad back, glad of its shelter. The tears,
even out of the wind, continued to trickle down
her cheeks for a while. This, in a way, was her
farewell to the stolen moments she had had
with Carl. This was the last time they would be
alone. From now on he could only be her
sister's fiancé, then her brother-in-law. She

wanted the night ride to go on for ever, but at
last they coasted silently, engine stilled, down
the slope of the apartment block. The sports car
stood there, boxes and parcels still piled on the
back seat.

Lisa got off the bike awkwardly, her legs stiff.
Carl put the machine on its stand and went at
once to inspect the car, combing hair from his
eyes with impatient fingers.

'She doesn't seem to have damaged it.' He
scooped some parcels from the seat, thrust them
at Lisa, picked up the rest himself, and led the
way upstairs.

The lounge light was on and the door was
slightly ajar. Carl tossed his parcels on to a patio
chair and walked into the room. Lisa dropped her
parcels beside his, and followed him.

Rachel, still wearing the cream trouser suit and
green scarf, was curled up on a divan, her
uncombed hair an explosion about her pale face.
A bottle stood on the table before her and a glass
was in her hand. Even with tear-stains below her
eyes she looked beautiful. Carl, unmoved, held
out his hand.

'The keys, Rachel.'

'Good grief, Mouse,' exclaimed Rachel in
stunned awe, 'what on earth are you wearing?'

'Clothes suitable for the back of a motor-bike,'
Carl said curtly. 'The keys!'

'What's the matter?' Her green eyes moved to
his face. 'Back so soon? Don't tell me she turned
you down after all, darling!'

'Shut up, Rachel!' his voice was harsh. 'Leave

Lisa out of this. And put that glass down, you know you're not a drinker.'

'What about you, Carl? Can you honestly tell me that you took photographs of her and you don't even find her attractive? Put your hand on your heart, my darling, and tell me that you don't like what you see when you look at my sister—be honest, for once.'

'Rachel!' Lisa burst out, but Carl motioned her to be quiet. He turned and looked her over slowly, his eyes studying every inch of her, seeming to ignore the wind-tossed hair, the shapeless clothing. She closed her own eyes, willed herself to stay where she was as his gaze burned deep.

'All right, I'll tell you,' he said at last, with cold finality. Lisa opened her eyes, and saw that he was intent on Rachel. 'I don't find your sister particularly attractive. I don't, in spite of what you think, lust after her. I don't care if I never see her again—and I don't care if I never see you again either. Get off my island, both of you, and get out of my life. And now that you've heard more than you want to hear—give me my car keys!'

Rachel fumbled in the pocket of her jacket, took the keys out, and threw them at Carl. She aimed for his face, but he caught the small bunch of keys easily before they found their mark.

'There are your precious keys!' she hissed at him. 'Now go and take your precious car back to your precious villa and——'

She jumped to her feet and for a moment it

looked as though the glass she held was going to follow the keys. But as Rachel moved, the liquid still in the glass spilled over on to her beautifully cut jacket. She stopped, horrified, and stared down at the spreading stain that darkened the material.

'Oh—damn!' Her voice broke on the last word. She looked up, her face suddenly childlike in its helplessness, then she dropped the glass and went blindly to Carl, reaching out for him, clutching him as though she would never let him go again, sobbing into his chest.

For a few seconds he stood motionless, then his arms went about her slowly and his head bent over hers. Unnoticed, Lisa went out of the room, down the stairs, and out on to the moonlight-silvered road.

The beach was completely deserted, the waves rolling in in big silent swells that loomed shorewards from the night, then broke gently and retreated with a hissing noise. Lisa would have liked to wade in and swim in the cool salty water, but her body ached with exhaustion and she didn't dare risk it. Instead she walked along the beach, her feet sinking into the soft sand.

Carl's look, his words, burned themselves into her mind as she walked. His rejection was nothing more than she deserved. It had to happen. But the deliberate cruelty of it hurt with a pain that almost destroyed her. She wanted to go to Mike, to be with him, but she didn't know where he lived. Besides, she could hardly burst in on him at that hour. There was only one place for

her to go to, and as exhaustion began to roll in on
her like the breakers on the beach, she turned
back towards the flat. A couple passed her as she
neared the road, and looked at her with open
surprise, and she suddenly remembered that her
hair was still tangled from the motor-bike
journey, and that she wore Carl's clothes, and she
was glad there was nobody else out and about to
see her.

Then thoughts about her appearance were
swept aside by a new fear. What if Carl was still
at the flat when she got back? What if he decided
to stay the night with Rachel? She tried hard not
to think of the two of them together, Rachel's
head on his shoulder, her long red hair tossed
across his brown chest, his arms about her—Lisa
dug her nails hard into her palms and walked
faster.

The car was gone, but the motor-bike was still
there. She wondered for a moment if Rachel had
gone back to the villa with Carl, but a light shone
beneath her sister's bedroom door.

Lisa pulled off Carl's clothes, stuffed them into
a cupboard out of sight, and attacked her hair
with a brush. It took a long time to get it under
control again, and to get ready for bed. When she
finally turned out the light, she fell asleep at
once, and dreamed about Carl.

CHAPTER TWELVE

RACHEL, wearing a black silk blouse and snug-fitting ivory slacks, was already in the kitchen when Lisa got up in the morning.

'It's my turn to make breakfast,' she said cheerily, and Lisa recognised the move as Rachel's way of making amends for the previous evening. Obviously everything had worked out for her sister. While Rachel bustled about in the kitchen Lisa took a shower and put on a simple sleeveless red dress with bronze flowers splashed over it. Then she combed her hair into its usual smooth style.

Carl's name wasn't mentioned during breakfast. Rachel had discovered that the food stocks were low, and as it wasn't one of Dorita's days Lisa volunteered to go to the village. She still wanted to see Mike, with his cheerful, reassuring grin, and a trip to the village gave her the ideal opportunity. Rachel wrote out a list in her flamboyant scrawl and settled down on the patio with a magazine and a bottle of nail polish.

'Darling, about Carl——' she said unexpectedly as Lisa was about to leave.

Lisa's heart gave a bound. 'Yes?'

'He's charming, when he wants to be—and you're such a vulnerable little mouse——'

'Rachel, we both told you last night that we don't even like each other very much!'

143

'I know you did, and I believe you,' Rachel protested, the green eyes wide and innocent. 'But I know that sometimes Carl—well, he tries out his charm now and then. I think that's what happened to poor Maria, if the truth was known. Carl was nice to her, and she thought it meant more than it did. I wouldn't want you to be hurt that way, Lisa.'

It was too late for warnings. Like a stupid mouse running headlong into a trap Lisa had already been caught and hurt. But she would never let Rachel find out.

'Don't worry about me, I know my limitations,' she said briskly. 'Besides, Carl loves you.'

'Yes.' Rachel's face lit up. 'Yes, he does. He was so—well, everything went well last night after he brought you home. I know how to handle him.'

'So you've fixed on a date?'

Rachel's eyes darkened, and she reached for the nail polish, suddenly losing interest in the conversation. 'There's plenty of time,' she said coolly.

As Lisa wandered round the little supermarket Rachel's words hung in letters of fire before her eyes, and Rachel's voice drowned out the chatter of other shoppers. She realised now that Rachel was afraid for the first time in her life. Afraid of losing Carl, afraid of being challenged by her younger sister. Just for a moment, on the patio, Lisa had glimpsed uncertainty flickering across Rachel's lovely face, when the wedding date was mentioned.

She paused in the act of lifting a bottle from a shelf. Poor Rachel! One of the tragedies of beauty was that it had to fade one day. A woman who could catch and hold any man with her looks must be haunted by the spectre of the future, the day when her beauty wouldn't be enough. And Rachel, coming back from Paris, expecting Carl to welcome her with open arms, had found that it wasn't as easy as that. She had seen the spectre moving towards her when Carl refused to play the game her way.

Lisa put the bottle carefully in her wire basket. She remembered Carl's angry voice saying, 'Who said I was going to marry your sister?' and she shivered. Carl must marry Rachel, he must make her happy. He couldn't just reject her and destroy her self-confidence. Lisa couldn't let that happen.

Mike was working in the dim depths of the shed at the harbour. As he looked up and saw her hesitating in the doorway his teeth gleamed in that heartwarming grin of his.

'Hi, come in and take a seat, if you can find one.'

She lifted a pile of papers from a stool and joined him at the workbench. 'Since you haven't come to me, I decided that I'd have to put pride aside and come to you,' she told him.

'I've been busy. I'm taking a party of holidaymakers out in an hour's time, but we can manage a drink before then. And I'll drive you back with these.' He indicated the shopping bags she had put down by the bench.

She watched him work in silence for a moment before saying, 'They had another terrible row last night.'

He shot-her a sidelong look. 'Don't let it get you down.'

'Mike, if Carl doesn't marry Rachel——'

'She'll find someone else,' he shrugged.

'Just like that?'

'It's easy for Rachel. Next time she might have the good sense to land her man and marry him right away instead of taking fright and rushing off to Paris.'

'Is that what happened?' she asked.

'That's my guess. She's never got this close to marriage before. She panicked.'

'But she came back,' Lisa said.

'But she gave Carl time to think. He's proud, he doesn't like to be taken for granted.'

'Will he forgive her?'

Mike shrugged. 'To tell you the truth, Lisa, I don't much care. Rachel has to learn to sort out her own problems, like the rest of us.'

'Why do you have to be so hard on her?'

'Because——' he stopped suddenly. After a moment he went on, 'Because I can't be bothered with beautiful people.'

'Doesn't that include Carl?'

Mike laughed. 'He's only one of the beautiful people as far as his money and his talent with a camera goes. Underneath he's as real as we are, I've told you that. Rachel turned his head when they met, but now she's given him a chance to think about about marriage. Oh, come on, let's get that drink.'

He got to his feet, but Lisa stayed where she was, suddenly swept by a wave of misery.

'Hey——' Mike tipped her chin up so that he could look at her, 'that row must have really bothered you. You look as though your world's just fallen in! Come on, tell Uncle Mike all about it.'

His kindness was too much for her. Tears suddenly filled her eyes, and she said, 'Oh— Mike!' then went into his arms, her face pressed tightly against his shoulder. He held her close, one hand stroking her hair.

'Nothing's ever as bad as that, love,' he murmured against her cheek. Lisa pushed herself back slightly so that she could look up into his steady grey eyes.

'Sorry——' she gave him a watery smile, and he returned it, then let his eyes wander over her face.

'Lisa, has anyone ever told you that you're lovely?' he asked softly, and bent to kiss her. She returned the kiss, tightened her arms about him, responded to the gentle but firm pressure of his lips on hers. As he finally lifted his head the bright oblong of light from the open door darkened, throwing Mike's downbent face into shadow. Lisa twisted in his arms to look at the doorway.

The man standing there was a black shape against the sunlight behind him, but as he stood motionless, hands on hips, feet planted apart, Lisa recognised him at once. There was no mistaking that broad-shouldered, slim-hipped outline. She could sense, rather than see, the dark eyes travelling over Mike and herself, still entwined together.

Mike was unconcerned. He let his embrace slacken but kept one arm around her. 'Hello, Carl.'

'I'm sorry to disturb you both at such a— delicate moment,' Carl's voice ripped through the shed like a wickedly sharp rapier. He took a step forward, ducking his dark head beneath the doorframe. 'I want the oars.'

'You didn't disturb anything,' Mike drawled. He released Lisa and moved forward to help Carl with the long oars which were stored on the rafters overhead. 'Taking the dinghy out?'

'I'm going fishing. Any objections?' Carl asked belligerently. He put the oars down, moved about the shed collecting a handline, hooks, bait, stuffing everything into a tattered rucksack he had picked up from a dark corner. At one point he came to stand before Lisa, staring down at her with angry eyes as he said icily, 'Could you please get out of my way?'

She stepped aside and he picked up a small box from the bench, then turned his broad back on her. She could feel his fury crowding the shed, pinning her against the bench.

Mike seemed to be unaware of Carl's anger. In the same lazy voice he said, 'Lucky you. I've got a group of tourists coming in later.'

'You seem to be having your own share of luck.' The meaning in Carl's voice, the way he looked from Mike to Lisa, was unmistakable. She

opened her mouth to protest, but Mike moved to
her side, put an arm about her, and said easily,
'You should know, Carl, that passers-by—or
droppers-in—don't always get the true picture.'

Carl glared at them both, started to say
something, then shrugged and slung the rucksack
over his shoulder. He picked up the oars as
though they weighed very little and walked out,
manipulating the long oars through the doorway
with practised ease.

'Now what's wrong with him?' Mike wondered
aloud, drawing Lisa to the door. They watched
Carl striding across the sand to where a bright
blue dinghy, the colour of his unbuttoned shirt,
lay above the waterline.

As he reached the dinghy and dropped the
rucksack into it with an agile flip of his shoulder a
thin boy wearing brief red trunks ran to him,
calling his name. Lisa recognised the youth who
had arrived on a motor-bike the day she came
across Carl painting the boat.

'Who's that?' she asked.

'Manuel—one of the kids who hang around the
harbour. He worships Carl.'

The boy was talking eagerly, gesturing with his
hands. Without looking at him Carl shook his
head, said something, and went on working on
the boat. Manuel stood where he was for a
moment before walking away slowly, shoulders
slumped, bare feet kicking the sand up in small
clouds before him.

'It looks as though Carl doesn't want any
company,' Mike said thoughtfully. Carl stripped

off the blue shirt and tossed it into the boat, together with his sandals. Then he began to roll up the legs of his black jeans. His naked back and arms gleamed in the sun as he moved. Watching him, yearning for him, Lisa realised how peaceful her holiday could have been if only Mike had been free to take her skin-diving. She would have spent most of her time with him, and Carl would never have had the chance to storm and charm his way into her heart.

Unaware of her thoughts and her gaze, he bent to grip the boat, pushing it easily over the soft sand to the sea. It dipped and rolled as it reached deeper water, then settled itself. He climbed aboard with ease, drops of water sparkling in the sun as they fell from his legs. Then he fitted the oars into the rowlocks and began to row with strong, steady strokes.

'What about that drink?' Mike remembered. 'I've still got time to run you home before I have to get back here.'

They went to the open-fronted restaurant Lisa had used before. From where she sat she could see the blue boat dancing over the waves, its tanned, lithe occupant bending to the oars, drawing them easily through the water, his naked torso flexing and stretching as he worked, his black hair blowing about his head.

Then the boat was turned parallel to the shore, and quickly disappeared from her sight.

'You didn't tell me why you were so unhappy,' Mike reminded her as they set off for the flat in his small car.

'Oh, I was just worried about Rachel. And feeling a bit sorry for myself.'

'In a place like this?' He nodded out of the car window at the blue sky, the white-walled little houses they were passing. 'How can you feel sad in Minorca?'

'Don't you ever feel sad?' The question was put lightly, but a shadow dimmed his smile for a brief moment.

'Not too often. My trouble is that I'm too damned stubborn to take happiness when it's within reach. I sometimes think I'm my own worst enemy. So——' the grin was back again as he glanced at her, '—I can't complain when things go wrong, can I?'

'Want to tell me about it?'

He shook his head. 'Thanks for the offer, but it isn't important.' Then they were at the apartment block and she hadn't time to ask him anything else.

Mike put the bags down on the patio. 'I'll have to rush back before my holidaymakers get impatient and hijack the boat. We need it for this afternoon's trip, remember?'

Lisa had forgotten. 'Mike——'

'I know. I wish we were going on our own, too. But keep smiling, I'll be right there beside you.' He bent and kissed her swiftly before hurrying back to his car.

Lisa picked up the bags and turned towards the open door. Rachel was standing inside the cool, dim lounge, watching her. Before Lisa could speak, her sister walked into her bedroom and closed the door firmly behind her.

Mike took them down to the harbour early in the afternoon. Carl, in crisp white shorts and matching short-sleeved shirt, was waiting for them in the boat.

As Lisa went down the harbour steps he put his hands on her waist and lifted her easily into the well of the boat.

'All right?' She nodded, the palms of her hands tingling from their brief encounter with his smooth brown chest, and turned away swiftly to study the boat. It was quite large, with a minute cabin. Most of the vessel was taken up by the open well, which had a padded bench all round it. In the centre of the well a low wall surrounded the glassed floor, and Lisa could see tiny agitated fish swarming beneath their keel.

Carl was lifting Rachel into the boat. She slid her hands deliberately inside his open shirt and up to his shoulders as he set her on her feet.

'Thank you, darling.' She reached up to kiss him as Mike jumped aboard and cast off. The boat eased away from the wall, with Carl at the wheel, and the little fish scattered as the engine stirred the water. The harbour's littered sandy bed gave way to rocks and gracefully waving seaweed as they moved into deeper water. Sunlight danced in patches over the seabed and fish glittered as they darted through its reflected light.

Rachel tossed her green and white robe aside, tied her long hair back, and stretched slim smooth-skinned legs along the seat to catch the sun. She wore a figure-hugging one-piece suit, and Lisa noticed that Mike's eyes lingered on her for a moment with genuine admiration before he turned to point out an unusual and beautiful rock formation sliding by beneath them.

Carl stared ahead, hands resting lightly on the wheel, legs astride. As Lisa watched him he shrugged off his shirt, flexing his back in the sun. He looked completely at home, and she could imagine him at the wheel of a sailing ship, the skull and crossbones flying above that dark curly head of his, a cutlass slung on his hip.

They anchored off the bay Mike had spoken about, a short stretch of sandy beach guarded by a cluster of multi-coloured rocks that partially hid it from view.

Rachel firmly refused to go into the water, but Lisa couldn't wait to strip off her blue teeshirt and shorts. She stepped lightly onto the gunwale and dived into the clear warm water, striking out for the beach as soon as her head broke surface. The rocks fronting the beach formed natural caves and archways and she swam in and out, feeling like a mermaid, her shadow trailing across the white sand below.

The final archway led to a small pocket of sand that was set slightly apart from the main stretch. Wringing water from her hair, Lisa waded out of the shallows and stepped onto a large flat rock, ideal for sunbathing. The boat was hidden from sight by a rocky wall. It was though she was alone on a desert island—alone for the first time since she had met Mike, she realised. She stretched out on the rock, savouring her solitude, and closed her eyes.

She was beginning to think, reluctantly, of swimming back to the others when Carl's voice said, 'So this is where you got to.'

He folded his long legs and dropped to the rock beside her. Water sparkled on his skin and in his hair.

'I was just going to swim back——'

'You can wait for a moment, can't you?' He put one hand on her shoulder and pushed her back as she started to sit up.

'Rachel——'

'Forget about her for a moment, can't you?' he asked angrily. 'She's got Mike for company. And I want to talk to you!'

CHAPTER THIRTEEN

THE secluded little bay that had seemed to be a refuge was now a trap. 'We don't have anything to talk about!'

'No? Don't you even want an apology?'

'I didn't expect one.'

'You're not going to get one. But I presumed that you felt I should grovel to you,' he went on casually. 'Why else would you be glaring at me and avoiding me? When I lifted you into the boat it was like holding a telephone pole. And I happen to know that you can yield when the mood takes you, so——'

His hand shot out and trapped her arm as she began to get up. She was forced to stay where she was, leaning over Carl as he lay on the rock. She tried not to notice how handsome he looked.

'You enjoyed them too—those stolen moments, little sister. What happened to turn you to ice?'

'Rachel happened. And I realised that all you wanted to do was to make her jealous, to punish her for leaving you!'

'I told you before——' there was just a touch of steel in his voice, '—to stop making my mind up for me. Why do you have to be so obsessed by this marriage?'

'That's what I came for in the first place. And——' she hesitated, looking down into the tanned face below her, concentrating all her attention on Rachel's happiness, 'Rachel loves you. Of course you're going to get married. That's what you both want.'

Carl released her arm and sat up, elbows on knees. His dark eyes stared past her shoulder, at the glittering sea.

'You know, when Mike introduced us I thought that Rachel was the most perfect woman I had ever seen. I wanted to spend the rest of my life with her,' he said, his voice husky. 'Now—I don't know. Was that love, little sister? Or was it just desire?'

'I don't know, I've——'

His eyes snapped back to her face. 'I know,' he said tightly, 'you've never been in love. You can tell others what to do, but you won't let anyone break down the wall you've built around your own emotions, will you? You won't ever get involved, will you, little sister?'

He was wrong, so wrong. But she could never tell him. She began to move, but he reached out for her, pushed her back on to the sun-warmed rock, his eyes hostile as they travelled over her.

'Since you're determined that we're going to be—what is it they call it? Kissing kin?—we'd better try the relationship out before it becomes official——'

Then his body was pinning hers to the rock, his lips held hers in a bruising, angry kiss, more of a punishment than a caress.

This time Lisa fought hard against the temptation to wrap her arms about his lithe body, to return his kisses passionately. She forced herself to lie still, her hands knotted into fists by her sides, her eyes shut tightly as his fingers tried to tease her body into a response.

When he finally released her she pushed him away as hard as she could. He grunted with surprise as he rolled to the edge of the rock, lost his balance, and toppled over on to soft sand. Before he could recover Lisa was running across the short strip of sand that led to the water. The soft stuff seemed to trap her toes at every step, but she finally reached the water and was knee-deep when Carl's fingers caught at her shoulders, spinning her round to face him. Sand powdered his damp body, and his eyes were slits of black glass.

'One day, little sister, you're going to annoy some man to breaking point, do you realise that? And when it happens, don't expect my sympathy!' he said breathlessly. Then he forced her head back and kissed her again, brutally, his arms crushing her against him, making a struggle pointless.

This time her longing to respond was too strong to be kept under control. She could feel his heart pounding, feel the silky warmth of his body against hers from their locked mouths to their toes. When he sensed that she had given in his lips became less demanding on her own, and his arms slackened slightly, allowing her to move her hands across his back, the sand gritty beneath her fingers. Then her mouth moved to his throat and chest as he lifted his head from hers. His mouth brushed her ear.

'I just wanted to prove to you, for the last time,' he whispered, 'that even an ice goddess can't help getting involved, if she's honest with herself.'

Lisa had forgotten how swift his reactions were. He still held her against him, but one hand whipped out and caught her wrist before her open palm reached his face. His fingers closed on her flesh like a vice, and his eyes were devoid of feeling as they looked down at her.

'All right, Lisa, you win,' he said coldly, then let her go and turned away, splashing through the archway and out into the sea beyond.

She rubbed her aching wrist, trying to understand what he meant. It seemed to her that she had lost—lost Carl, lost her self-respect, and certainly she had lost the opportunity to put Rachel's interests first.

Slowly she waded beneath the archway. The boat bobbed at anchor a short distance away, and Carl's dark head and brown arms moved through the sea towards it with a steady rhythm. Lisa kept her feet on the sandy bottom until she was waist-deep in the water, then let herself fall forward into its embrace, and struck out for the boat.

Carl reached a tanned arm down to her as she reached it, and lifted her on board without any apparent effort. He picked up two towels, tossed one to Lisa, and turned away from her.

Mike was stretched out on the roof of the cabin, eyes closed, face turned to the sun. In the well of the boat Rachel was turning the pages of a magazine with swift sharp movements that showed anger. Lisa shivered under the warm sun, wondering if her absence and Carl's was the cause of her sister's annoyance. Then she saw the green eyes flick in Mike's direction and realised by the look in them that Mike was the cause of Rachel's rage.

'Darling, give me that——' Rachel's voice was honeyed as she took the towel from Carl and started to dry his back. 'Where have you two been?' she asked casually.

'Exploring—and talking.' Carl turned and looked down at her as she caressed his chest with the towel.

She looked up at him. 'Talking about what?'

He took the towel from her, tossed it aside. 'About you—what else? Lisa's very anxious to see us happily married before she goes home, aren't you, Lisa? So I thought Friday might be a suitable day. What do you think?'

Rachel took a step back, eyes wide. Lisa went on drying her arms, though time seemed to stop for her. Now she knew what Carl had meant when he said, 'You've won.'

'Friday?' she heard Rachel say, weakly. 'Well, I——'

Mike sat up, swinging his legs over the side of the cabin. 'Well, well—congratulations, Rachel!' He jumped down and put his hands on Rachel's shoulders. She deliberately turned her head so that his kiss landed on her cheek. 'You're supposed to congratulate the man,' she pointed out coldly, 'not the woman.'

'I know, but I still feel that I should say—

congratulations, Rachel,' he said smoothly, then turned to Carl, hand outstretched. 'And you too, Carl!'

Carl's eyes were fixed on Rachel. 'I haven't been accepted yet.'

'But I'm sure you will be,' Mike said heartily. 'Right, Rachel?'

There was a brief pause, then Rachel said, in a stronger voice, 'Of course he is! I was—I just didn't expect you to name the day so suddenly, darling. Oh, Carl——!' She moved into his arms and lifted her face for his kiss. Mike tipped Lisa's face to his and dropped a light kiss on her lips.

'The bridesmaid and best man deserve to be congratulated too. We're finally going to come in handy!'

'If you're quite sure, Rachel——' Carl's deep voice said from behind Lisa.

'Of course I'm sure! It's what we planned, isn't it?'

'Before you went off to Paris,' he said dryly, and Lisa turned away from Mike in time to see Rachel's face darken with anger.

'Carl! Don't start that again—I told you, I just had pre-wedding nerves. It's over, I'm not going to get them again!'

'I hope not. Because I'm not going to cancel the wedding a second time. This time, Rachel, you have to go through with it.'

'I can't wait till Friday!' Rachel's anger vanished, and she smiled up at him. 'Oh, darling, let's all go out tonight and celebrate!'

'So—we're going to be related by the time you

leave Minorca.' Carl moved to Lisa. His hands
landed lightly on her shoulders, and before she
could turn her head away his lips had brushed
hers in a brief kiss that was enough to set her
body on fire again. When he straightened up
there was no sign in his face that the kiss had
affected him at all. He looked down at her as
though she was a stranger.

During the trip back to the harbour, and
throughout the evening they spent in a restaurant
high above Mahon's lights, Lisa tried to keep
telling herself that everything was working out
the way she wanted. But as she ate and laughed
and danced there was an ache in her heart that
refused to go away.

When Rachel, beautiful in a gauzy black pants
suit with narrow shoulder straps and a low bodice
embroidered in turquoise, said, 'Mouse, when
you come to visit us I'm going to take you to
some marvellous shops and I'm going to buy you
some decent clothes——' Lisa nodded, smiled,
and knew she would never be able to visit Rachel
and Carl. She couldn't risk the pain. No use
telling herself that she hadn't lost him, because
she had never had the right to find him in the
first place. It was too late to think of that.

Carl himself, in white evening sweater and
black suit, rarely looked at her. He devoted
himself to Rachel, and Lisa was taken aback
when, towards the end of the evening, he stood
up and held his hand out to her.

'Come on, little sister, we should have one
dance together.'

They drifted round the floor in silence for a while before he finally said, 'You look very lovely tonight.'

She bit her lip. 'Beside Rachel?'

His fingers tightened on hers, his voice was suddenly angry. 'Yes, beside Rachel! Can't I ever offer you a compliment without being corrected? You suit green, you look lovely—please, just for once stop being her sister and be a woman in your own right! And why aren't you looking happier?' he went on. 'You should be very happy. You've got what you wanted.'

His hand seemed to burn through the back of her dress, and the knowledge that if she looked up she would see his mouth close to hers made her falter and miss a step. His arm immediately tightened about her, holding her until she regained her balance.

'Lisa, if Rachel cared about your happiness as much as you care about hers, you'd be very fortunate, you know that?'

'Do you mind if we sit down?' she asked desperately, but he shook his head.

'Not just yet—though I know you'd far rather dance with Mike than with me. But I want to ask you to do something for me, Lisa.'

'What could I do for——'

'Shut up and listen! The other night, when we had dinner at the villa, I told you about my father's farm, remember? Since then I've——' He stopped speaking. Looking up, she saw that he was staring over her head, his mouth tight.

'What is it?' she queried.

His arms dropped to his sides. 'Maria and Eduardo. They're speaking to Rachel.' He started to push his way from the crowded dance floor, dragging Lisa after him by the wrist.

'What did you want me to do?' she reminded him.

'I think I've left it too late,' Carl said grimly, then let Lisa's hand go as they reached the table.

It was obvious from the triumphant sparkle in Rachel's eyes and the hard glitter in Maria's that Rachel had told the others about the wedding date. Eduardo shook Carl's hand warmly and Maria kissed him, winding her white arms about his neck possessively. It was Carl who ended the kiss.

'You must invite us to the ceremony, of course—and you must allow us to hold a party for you afterwards,' Maria enthused, her smile brilliant as she turned it on Lisa. 'My dear, how delighted you'll be to see your sister and Carl marrying!' Her eyes were inquisitive, watching for a sign of weakness. Lisa made sure that her answering smile was just as brilliant.

'Perhaps we'll see more of you, Carlos, when you're a married man and settled here on the island,' Eduardo added.

Carl began to speak, a muscle twitching in his jaw, but Rachel's voice chimed out, clearer than his, 'We won't live on the island, but we'll be here from time to time, of course.'

There was a brief silence. Lisa saw Eduardo look at Carl with a question in his eyes, then the older man nodded slightly and put his hand on his wife's arm. 'Maria, we'll have to go back to our friends' table now.'

Maria, too, had seen the quick look that passed between the brothers. Lisa could tell by the sudden realisation in the Spanish woman's eyes. But instead of letting her husband draw her away she said sweetly, 'But, Rachel, of course you're going to live on Minorca! At Cadala. Where else would you live?'

'Where?' Rachel's face was puzzled. Carl sighed, raised his eyes to the ceiling, as he had done when Lisa appeared at the bedroom door in the villa. Maria's eyes narrowed slightly.

'Do you mean that Carlos hasn't told you yet? Then he must have planned it as a wedding gift— a lovely surprise for you, yes?'

'Yes, Maria,' Carl's voice was light, but there was a chill in its depths. 'But you love telling secrets, don't you?'

'Maria, our friends are waiting,' Eduardo insisted, and this time she went with him, casting one final triumphant smile at Carl and Rachel.

'Come and dance——' Mike gathered Lisa into his arms and whisked her on to the dance floor. Just before the crowd closed around them Lisa caught a glimpse of Rachel's face, drawn and angry.

'Maria's always been a troublemaker,' Mike steered Lisa to the other side of the dance floor, 'and she knows exactly what she's doing.'

'Do you know what she was talking about?'

'More or less. Eduardo got a nice piece of farmland from his father when the bulk of the land was sold. The tenant farmer living in the cottage that went with it was getting on in years, and Eduardo decided to let him farm it, and to sell it to the builders when the old fellow retired. Carl's had his eye on it for a while, and the other night Eduardo agreed to sell it to him. Carl plans to modernise the cottage and farm the land himself.'

Lisa stared up at him. 'But Rachel would never agree to that!'

'He stopped talking about it when she appeared. But when she went off to Paris, I guess that did it—he just went ahead and closed the deal.'

'Does he seriously expect her to go along with it?'

'I think he's pretty determined now. She's gone too far—we both heard her say that this time the marriage was going ahead, no matter what. The farm's the "what", I suppose.' Mike swung her round in a neat turn, grinned down at her. 'Only Rachel didn't know about that when she said yes on the boat this afternoon.'

'That's deceitful!'

'So is going to Paris on a non-existent assignment. Let's face it, Lisa, your sister and Carl are a better match than we thought.'

And Carl, Lisa realised as the music stopped, had been about to ask her to sweeten Rachel into accepting the idea of the farm. Anger rose up in her as she realised that he had intended to use her again.

Rachel and Carl weren't at the table when they got back to it.

'Well, that's that.' Mike said easily. 'Shall we go and do the rounds? This place is too grand for me. I know some very good dives.'

'What about the others?'

'My guess is that Rachel's walked out in a rage, and Carl's followed her. I'd have left her to find her own way home, if I'd been him. Forget about them, let's enjoy ourselves instead.'

As she allowed him to lead her out of the restaurant Lisa doubted if she would be able to enjoy any part of her holiday again. But Mike refused to let her talk about Rachel, and concentrated on making sure that the rest of the evening was carefree, filled with laughter and music. With his encouragement, Lisa began to relax and have a wonderful time.

It was very late when he finally announced that he was going to take her home.

'I have to do some work on one of the boats early in the morning,' he told her. 'And you should get some sleep.'

'I won't get a chance if Carl and Rachel are throwing tantrums in the flat,' she remembered uneasily as he drove through the night.

He stopped the car by the side of the road and turned her to face him. 'Lisa, forget about Rachel's moods. She goes her own way and nobody's allowed to cross her. You shouldn't let her get to you the way she does.'

'I was brought up with her, remember?' she asked wryly.

'It's time somebody made her toe the line!' Mike's voice was fast, angry. 'I should have done it myself, when——' He stopped abruptly.

'When what?'

'Nothing,' he said gruffly, without looking at her. He leaned forward to switch on the ignition, but Lisa put her hand on his, stopping him. All at once an idea was beginning to form in her mind.

'Rachel came here on holiday. You introduced her to Carl. She'd already met you in England. Mike, was she here to see you? Were you and Rachel——?'

'We thought so. At least, I thought so, but then I'm pretty stupid at times!' he said in a low, hard voice.

'What happened?'

He turned to look at her. In the car's interior she couldn't make out his face, but she could hear the pain in his voice. 'What always happens with your sister? When we first met she turned on the usual charm, made me feel that I was the only man in the world. Oh, Rachel really knows how to do that! Then she had to go off to the other side of the world to work, and I came here. We kept in touch, and when she was free she came for a holiday, to be with me. I really thought that——' he stopped, slammed his hand against the steering wheel. 'But you know Rachel. She started laying down rules. I had to put her career first, I had to take some jackass executive job she'd heard of, then we'd be able to jet everywhere together and be sensational people envied by thousands. I was supposed to put her on a pedestal and worship her!' He laughed shortly. 'Worship her? I was head over heels in love with her—I was crazy about her. But that wasn't enough. I had to let her change me. And that was where it all started to go wrong. I wouldn't change. I wanted a real wife, someone who'd treat me like a human being and not a suitable escort. We were just beginning to realise that it was going sour when Carl came back from an assignment somewhere. I introduced him to Rachel—he thought she was just a casual friend of mine—and on went the charm for him. That's when I realised that it hadn't been genuine for me,' he added bitterly. 'Carl fell for it, and for her. Who wouldn't?'

'Is she marrying him just to spite you?'

Mike stared at her in the darkness. 'Rachel? She'd never do that. She didn't care enough about me to want to make me jealous anyway. No, she just found someone willing to do things her way, that's all.'

'And now?'

'Now I think I'll move on,' he said slowly. 'Not because my partner and the woman I love are getting married. I could live with that—I've managed so far. I've just got itchy feet. I've been thinking of it for a while. The Greek islands, Portugal—there are a lot of places I haven't seen yet. This seems as good a time as any to make the move.'

'Mike, I'm sorry.'

He laughed, and kissed the end of her nose. 'Nothing to be sorry about. I'm just too pigheaded and Rachel's too beautiful. That's the way things work out sometimes. Come on, I'll take you home.'

To Lisa's relief the road in front of the apartments was empty. Mike stopped the car. 'I'll not come in, it's too late. Lisa, if my itchy feet take me back to England some time could I drop in and say hello?'

'I hope you will,' she told him sincerely.

'Perhaps we could get to know each other properly, away from Minorca,' he said quietly. 'You know something? I wish I'd met you before I met Rachel.' Then he leaned forward, opened the passenger door for her, and kissed her gently on the lips. 'Or I wish Rachel could have been more like you.'

The flat was in darkness, but Rachel's high-heeled sandals and the jacket of her pants suit lay on the lounge floor, where she had tossed them down.

'Mouse, you haven't got anything planned for this morning, have you?' she asked casually when Lisa arrived back from her the pool on the following day.

'I thought I might take a bus somewhere. It's time I saw more of the island.'

'Why don't you come with us? Carl's taking me to see this silly farmland he's bought. I'd like you to see it too,' Rachel added quickly as Lisa opened her mouth to protest. 'Call it moral support, if you like. Please?'

'If Carl wants to own farmland it's none of my business,' Lisa objected uneasily.

Rachel waved an impatient hand. She was looking fresh and natural in a white peasant-style dress splashed with brightly coloured flowers, her hair tied back loosely.

'I'm not asking you to get involved, I just want your company. Carl's just got a bee in his bonnet about his family, and its history. It's a hang-up and I suppose I'll have to put up with it for the moment.'

'I don't think it's a hang-up.'

'You wouldn't, would you?' said Rachel with the indulgence an adult might show towards a young child. 'But I've been thinking—it wouldn't hurt to go along with it just now. The house needs rebuilding, according to him, and by the time that's done he'll have lost interest in the whole idea!'

CHAPTER FOURTEEN

'AND if he hasn't?' Lisa persisted.

Rachel's eyebrows rose. 'Then I'll have to think of some way to change his mind. I'm certainly not going to live in a farmhouse! Besides, once we're married—oh, for goodness' sake, Mouse, go and get ready. He'll be here soon!'

Carl arrived just as Lisa emerged from her room. His eyes flickered without interest over her striped tee-shirt and dark green slacks, and he only nodded when Rachel, after greeting him warmly, announced that Lisa was going with them to see the land.

They drove across the island, taking the broad modern roads at first, then turning on to small local roads. The sea appeared before them, dark blue receding to a hazy band along the horizon, here and there dotted with yacht sails. The car went along a shore road, past high fawn rocks pitted with the caves that earlier Minorcans had lived in, then turned inland slightly again, through small neat fields bordered with rough-stone walls.

Lisa sat alone in the back seat, watching Carl's strong tanned hands on the steering wheel, and the sun teasing lights from the thick black hair that curled to the nape of his neck. Once or twice their eyes met in the driving mirror and she moved her gaze away each time, afraid that he might see unguarded longing in her face.

Then the car turned up a long lane, and stopped in front of a low white farmhouse.

'The place is empty now.' Carl got out, pulled the driving seat forward to let Lisa out, and went round to open Rachel's door. 'The old couple moved to Alayor, to live with their married daughter. One of the neighbouring farmers looks after things just now. He's agreed to give me a hand here, and to keep an eye on the place when I have to be away.'

'So you intend to leave occasionally?' Rachel got out of the car and stood looking at the cottage and the surrounding fields.

'I'll have to take on photographic assignments.' Carl didn't seem to notice the thinly-veiled sarcasm in her voice. 'There's not enough land here to support us—at least, not in the style you'd demand, Rachel. But I'll stay on the island as much as possible.'

'And what about me?'

'You'll be with me. You won't be taking on so much work, either, once we're married,' he said blithely. Without waiting for her reaction he produced a key and strode forward to unlock the door for them, standing aside to let them go in before him. He wore a gold-coloured shirt and tailored, smart dark brown trousers, and Lisa noticed how well he blended in with his background—as always. But she couldn't imagine Rachel, fragile and graceful in the white dress with white sandals, as a farmer's wife.

She followed her sister into the cottage's dim
interior and waited as Carl opened shutters and
windows, talking as he moved about.

'Of course it's small and fairly basic just now,
but it's a good building. It can be extended and
modernised, and it should be quite easy to follow
the original lines of the house and avoid turning
it into a monstrosity—like the villa,' he added
with contempt. As they followed him from one
room to another, Lisa could see the finished
house as Carl described it in a voice rich with
enthusiasm. Walls were going to be knocked
down to make larger rooms, to make way for
huge windows, and an extension that would allow
a modern kitchen and another bedroom. When
they went back outside and walked around the
building she could see that his rough plans
already made the most of the lovely views from
the area—the sea in front, a range of low
colourful hills to one side.

Rachel said very little, but her face, as they
went back outside, had an expression of disbelief.
While Carl and Lisa walked round the cottage,
she went to the car, huddling into the passenger
seat like a wounded white bird. Carl paid no
attention.

'Well, little sister?' he asked as he locked the
cottage door.

'I can see that it's going to be lovely,' admitted
Lisa.

'I had been thinking about it for months,
trying to persuade Eduardo to sell to me.' He
leaned against the sturdy white wall, looking

already like a man with his own home. He had never been so relaxed with the villa. 'Then the other night, when I talked about the farm, and you were interested, I almost told you—you think I've done the right thing?'

'For you, yes. But not for Rachel.'

His eyes were shuttered again. 'My wife will live in my house,' he said with finality. 'You were the one who was so anxious that I should go ahead and marry Rachel.'

'But you didn't tell me about this place!'

The car horn tooted.

'I tried,' he reminded her, 'but you wouldn't listen.'

'Carl, it isn't fair to spring this place on Rachel! You have to give her time to get used to the idea, that's all!'

'My home will be here, in Cadala,' he said coldly. 'And since Rachel has given me her firm promise, her home will also be here—in Cadala!'

The horn tore the summer's day with another harsh blast of sound and he walked away, leaving Lisa to trail along at his back. He didn't look, or sound, as though the farm was just a craze, as Rachel had said.

Obviously his determination had got through to Rachel as well. She said very little during the drive back, but that afternoon, when they were both at the pool, she said suddenly, 'If Carl really thinks that I'm going to bury myself in the back of beyond after we're married, he's wrong!'

She was stretched out on a lounger, her superb figure shown off to advantage in a deep blue bikini. Lisa towelled her shoulders and pulled off her bathing cap.

'Wait and see. The house is going to be gorgeous.'

'I don't care if it's a palace, I'm not going to live on this island! I don't expect him to live in England, do I? So why should I be expected to live here?' Rachel pushed her sunglasses to the top of her red head, and glared.

All at once Lisa wondered if she would be able to keep going until the wedding without slapping Rachel's lovely, selfish face.

'Why on earth,' she asked bluntly, 'are you marrying him?'

Rachel dragged her gaze from a group of tanned young men who had smiled at her on their way past. 'Why? Why does anyone get married, Lisa?'

'For love?'

'Of course. And security. And besides, I always said I'd get married when I reached twenty-five. It's the right age for marriage.'

'And so you picked the right sort of husband.'

Rachel didn't notice the sarcasm in the statement. 'Carl adores me, he's wealthy—or he was before he decided to throw away money on this farm! He's good-looking, and he's available— honestly, darling, in my world it's rare to meet a man like Carl who's still single. Let's go back to the flat, it's too hot here.'

She got to her feet in one smooth movement that attracted the gaze of every man and youth in or around the pool, and set off, leaving Lisa to collect magazines, sun-tan lotion, and towels.

'And what about Carl's feelings?' she persisted when she was following Rachel up the steps to the flat.

'What about them? He's very happy, and so he should be. I'd say he's getting a bargain. I can't imagine him settling down with some local girl, can you? Take Maria, for instance. Not bad-looking just now, but in a few years she'll have a weight problem. I won't. And she'll probably be a shrill-voiced nag.'

Lisa draped her damp towel over the patio wall. 'I was talking about what matters to Carl,' she said levelly. 'Minorca, and the land he's bought back, saved from the builders. He loves the island, he wants to live here, Rachel.'

Rachel's full red mouth hardened into a line. 'Mouse, I've told you—he'll forget about the farm once the novelty's worn off!' she snapped, wriggling seductively into the blue beach dress that matched her bikini. 'I'm getting more than a little tired of your wide-eyed attitude towards everything, and the way you keep rushing to Carl's defence. You're my sister, remember? You're supposed to see my point of view!'

'Not if I don't agree with it!'

Rachel slipped her shoes on, then looked up, eyes narrowed. 'Funny, I never used to be wrong all the time. We never disagreed, not until I left you and Carl on this island together,' she said slowly. 'You've changed since then, Mouse. What happened to you?'

Lisa felt her face colour under the cool green stare. 'I'm older, that's all.'

'I wonder. Perhaps Maria saw more than she told me, that night when she found you both alone at the villa.'

'Don't start all that again! You know perfectly well that Carl only took me skin-diving as a favour to Mike. And if I'd known what a fuss it was going to cause, I would never have gone!' she added, with all her heart. But Rachel's suspicion had been tossed aside as a new idea struck her.

'Mike! That's who I should talk to! He could persuade Carl to give up this crazy idea about being a farmer. Do you think he's at the harbour now?'

'Why should he try to influence Carl?'

Rachel stopped, one hand on the gate, 'Because of the partnership, of course,' she said triumphantly. 'If Carl's farming, he can't work with Mike. It's in Mike's interests to help me talk Carl out of it.'

'But it won't make any difference to Mike! He's leaving Minorca anyway!'

Rachel, already on her way down the steps, stopped and turned. 'What did you say?'

Lisa bit her lip. 'I should have left it to him to tell Carl when he was ready. Mike's giving up his share of the business and leaving Minorca.'

Rachel came back to the patio, her eyes wide and bright. 'When?'

'Quite soon. He says he feels restless.'

'But he can't! He can't just—just go like that!' Rachel's voice shook slightly. 'What am I going to do without him?'

'You don't need him,' Lisa said reasonably. 'Carl does.'

'But——' Rachel caught at Lisa's arm, 'but he might not come back, Mouse! I need to know that he's here, that I can see him!'

'Why should he stay here, when you won't?'

'Don't keep asking silly questions!' her sister blazed at her. 'You don't understand! I—I don't want Mike to go away! I—I—can't——'

She sat down on one of the chairs as though her knees had given way, and stared up at Lisa. 'What am I going to do?' she asked again, and Lisa suddenly understood what her sister meant. She sat on the other chair, took Rachel's hand in hers. It was cold and trembling.

'Rachel, are you in love with Mike?'

Rachel's face had paled beneath its faint tan and tears stood in her eyes, diamonds against emeralds. 'Of course I don't love him!' her voice recovered. 'How could I? I just—just don't want him to go away, that's all. Lisa, I want to know that I can see him, talk to him——'

'That's love,' Lisa said wryly.

'It can't be!' Rachel blinked and the tears glittered in the sunlight as they rolled down her lovely face. 'I could never love someone as selfish and as stubborn as Mike! He's impossible! He's—he's——'

'But you followed him to Minorca.'

Rachel pulled her hand free and scrubbed it over her face, smearing the tears away. 'I must have been mad. But in England he'd been—it was wonderful. I thought it would go on like that.

Then I came here and realised what he was really like!' she added sullenly, her mouth turning down at the corners.

'What was he really like?'

Rachel got up, pacing the patio angrily as she talked. 'Completely selfish! If we got married, I'd be his wife—he made me sound like a possession, Mouse! He wanted me to make a home for him, to put him before my work. It was ridiculous! Then Carl came, and he was different—understanding, just right for me——'

'Did you agree to marry him to teach Mike a lesson?'

'No!' Rachel stared down at her, shocked. 'Carl was my sort of person—before this farm nonsense started! And Mike didn't really care what happened to me. If he had he'd have fought for me, wouldn't he? But he didn't!' her voice was bitter again.

'What about Paris?' asked Lisa.

Rachel ran a hand through her hair. 'I didn't know what to do, Mouse! I thought that if I went away for a few days Mike might stop being so stubborn. He might have come after me, but he didn't. Then I knew that I was doing the right thing, marrying Carl.'

'Poor Carl!' Lisa said wryly.

'What does that mean?'

'Falling in love with someone who really wants his partner.'

'There you go again, Mouse!' Rachel's tears were a thing of the past as she stood over Lisa. 'I told you—I don't want Mike! I never wanted him—not on his terms. I'm very happy about marrying Carl. I just——'

'You just want Mike there, on a string.' Lisa had never thought she could dislike her sister so much.

'No!' Rachel's eyes blazed at her. 'I think Carl's got enough to think about just now without losing Mike's support as well. I'm going to talk Mike out of going. If Carl arrives tell him—tell him I'm getting my hair done, or something!' And before Lisa could say another word Rachel had gone.

Lisa stripped off her damp swimsuit and put on a yellow shirtwaister. As she brushed her hair she told herself to stop worrying about Rachel. If her sister started trouble between Carl and Mike, it was their business, not Lisa's. Carl was an experienced man, and if he chose to marry a woman who didn't really love him, that was his lookout. Rachel would make an ideal hostess, a decorative wife. Perhaps that was what Carl wanted. And Mike could take care of himself.

Whatever happened, she decided as she put on some lipstick and perfume, she would keep out of it. She had had her fingers well and truly burned, and she had learned her lesson. Then before she knew it she was locking the door, running down the stairs and along the dusty road after Rachel.

Although she never walked when she could avoid it Rachel had travelled at a good speed. She was striding past the little supermarket, almost at the harbour, when Lisa caught up with her.

'Rachel——' she gasped, 'I think you should

take time to think things out before you say
anything to Mike——'

Rachel's red hair brushed her bare shoulders as
she shook her head. 'I've thought it all out. I only
need to make it clear to him that Carl needs him,
that's all.' She turned and flashed a bright,
mechanical smile at Lisa as they reached the
harbour. 'Don't look scared, Mouse. I won't
make a fool of myself,' she said, and her voice
was as brittle as her smile.

The glass-bottomed boat was moored by the
harbour, and the shed door was open. Mike
appeared in the doorway as they went across the
sand. He was wearing a black tee-shirt and faded
blue denims, and his brown hair was untidy. He
grinned his wide warm grin when he saw them
both, and Rachel's step faltered.

'Welcome to my parlour—sorry it's in a mess,'
he wiped his hands on a rag as he led them into
the shed. A smear of oil decorated his cheek.
'Carl isn't here, Rachel.'

'I came to see you.' She stood well away from
the cluttered workbench. 'Lisa says you're
leaving. I think you should stay—for Carl's sake,'
she said bluntly.

'Did he ask you to come here?'

'No. But I think it's perfectly obvious that he
can't manage this place without you. You'll have
to stay!'

Mike's face hardened, and he tossed the rag on to
the bench. 'Sorry, Rachel, your high-handed
attitude won't work with me. I've already found a
good replacement to run the place for Carl. Young

Manuel's brother's getting married. He needs the job, he's good with boats. Carl won't miss me.'

'That's not the point! You have no right to—to just walk out on him!'

'Tough. But he should be getting used to that sort of treatment by now,' Mike said coldly, and for a minute Lisa thought her sister was going to fly at him.

'You!' she almost spat the words at him. 'You're a——' She paused, and Mike said,

'I know what I am, Rachel. And who I am. Come on, I'll buy you both a coffee.'

'Mike!' Rachel's voice stopped him as he walked out of the shed. Her fingers twisted nervously round each other. 'Mike—don't go.'

'I'm a free agent, Rachel. I'm going.'

'Then——' said Rachel in a ragged, uncertain voice, '—I'm coming with you.'

'You're what?' He turned to stare at her, just as Lisa protested,

'Rachel, you can't! What about Carl!'

'No, thanks, Rachel, I'm travelling alone from now on,' Mike said harshly. But she crossed the space between them, caught at his arm and spun him to face her.

'I'm coming with you, Mike Barclay, whether you like it or not,' she said shakily. 'Even if it means living on that nasty little boat of yours— even if it means being miserable for the rest of my life. Whatever happens, you're never going to get away from me again!'

He stared at her, mistrust in his face. 'Rachel,

if this is one of your crazy stunts—and keep away from me, you'll get oil all over your dress!'

But Rachel kept going, right into his arms, her face pressed tightly against his shoulder. 'Who cares about oil?' she said in a muffled voice. 'Just—just take me back to the flat and tell me where we're going and when we're leaving—on any terms you want, you stubborn, impossible— oh, Mike!'

The mistrust gave way to astonishment, then to a tenderness that transformed his face as slowly, gently, he put his arms about Rachel, holding her as though she was a very precious, very fragile treasure.

CHAPTER FIFTEEN

It wasn't until she was stepping into Mike's little car that Rachel remembered. She turned a tear-stained, oil-smeared face to Lisa and Mike.

'Carl! I'll have to tell Carl!'

'We'll tell him together,' Mike said firmly. 'Coming back to the flat with us, Lisa?'

'I have shopping to do,' she lied, and watched them drive off together. She wandered round the streets, staring into shop windows without seeing anything, trying to come to terms with the latest developments.

She had never seen Rachel so happy, had never seen her sister's eyes look at a man with such open adoration. They seemed an oddly assorted couple, and yet Lisa was quite certain that they would be happy together.

As for Carl—she tried not to think of how he was going to be rejected for a second time. But it was better than being trapped in marriage with Rachel, when all the time her heart belonged to Mike. Carl would have to get over it, just as she herself was going to have to get over losing him. She would go home and settle into her usual routine, and Carl—he would have his farm to keep him occupied.

She glanced at her watch and decided it was time to go back to the flat to find out what Rachel and Mike planned to do. They would probably

leave the island soon. There would be packing to
see to, and while she was about it, Lisa decided,
she might as well try to arrange an earlier flight
home.

She looked up from the paving-stones at her
feet—and saw Carl swing round the corner
ahead and come towards her. Her heart thudded
an alarm and she looked desperately round for a
hiding place. Carl's head lifted and his pace
quickened as he saw her. Just then Lisa realised
that she was beside the little supermarket.
Ignoring his shout, she whisked into the shop.
It was almost empty, and she snatched up a
wire basket and scuttled to the rear of the
building, where she could hide among the
stacked shelves.

The door opened and shut. Lisa studied the
pile of tins inches from her nose and selected one
without looking at the label with its picture of the
contents.

'There you are,' said Carl's deep voice from
behind her. His blue-sleeved arm reached out
and took the basket from her. She had no option
but to turn and look up at him. His face was
unsmiling. 'I've been looking for you.'

'Have you seen——'

'Yes, I've seen Rachel,' he cut in. 'I went to the
flat to talk to my fiancée about our wedding
plans, and I found her locked in my best friend's
arms.'

She put one hand out to him, but drew it back
before he could reject it himself. 'Carl, I'm so
sorry.'

He ignored her. 'When we finally got around to general adult conversation she told me that you were in the village somewhere. So I thought I'd find you and tell you about the arrangements I've been making for the wedding.'

'Carl, I know it's going to be very difficult for you, having to cancel the wedding again, but there's nothing else you can do,' she said, unable to find the right words. 'Yes, people are going to gossip, but that won't last for ever——'

His eyes seemed to bore right into her soul. 'Little sister, I have no intention of cancelling anything. I thought I made that clear when Rachel agreed to marry me on Friday.'

'But you can't insist on going through with it!' He must, surely, be joking, and yet the dark eyes looking down on her were quite empty of humour.

'Naturally I'm going to insist. I have every right to insist. There will be no cancellation!'

Lisa flared into anger. 'That's monstrous! You can't do it! Rachel and Mike love each other!'

'So I believe. However, I live on this island. I was born here and I come from a well-known local family. I have no wish to become a laughing-stock among my own people. That's why,' he ended deliberately, 'I'm getting married, as arranged, on Friday.'

'Of all the arrogant, cruel, selfish——!' she spluttered for words to describe him.

'I expect I am,' Carl agreed levelly. He looked at the solitary tin in the basket he held. 'Is that all you're buying? Asparagus tips? Where's your well-known efficiency? Your love of organising? Why not try this—and some of this—and these——?' He scooped tins and packets from the shelves, dropped them into the basket. The gold chain at his throat glinted as he moved about. Then he stopped and swung round on Lisa, brows drawing together over his dark eyes.

'I don't quite see where you fit in, little sister, but it seems to me that you've managed to confuse everyone since you came to Minorca. If you hadn't been here, I have a feeling that Rachel wouldn't have tried to get out of our marriage on Friday,' he challenged.

Lisa swallowed nervously, backing away. 'Can't you see that the marriage would never have worked out?'

He brushed her words aside with a wave of one hand. 'So as I see it, it's up to you to make amends.'

'But I—what can I do?'

'You mean that that know-it-all brain of yours hasn't worked out the answer yet? I thought of it as soon as I saw Rachel and Mike together and knew that I wasn't the only man in her life.' He took something else from a shelf and dropped it into the basket. 'You bullied me into setting a new date. You were probably the one who threw Rachel into Mike's arms——'

'I did not!'

'So it's up to you to take her place. Cancel your flight home and buy something suitable for the wedding. I'll see to everything else.'

He strode away along an aisle as though the

matter was settled and there was nothing more to say. Lisa stood where she was and gaped at his back, her mind numb with shock. When she caught up with him he was at the check-out, unloading an unlikely assortment of goods from the basket.

'Carl, I——!' she stopped as she saw the inquisitive look the cashier was giving them both. Carl packed the goods from the basket into a paper container and the cashier named a sum. Lisa fumbled for her purse, then stared into it, unable to concentrate on what she was doing.

'Give it to me——' Carl's hand reached out, took the purse from her unresisting fingers. He handed money over and gave the purse back to her.

'Now that you're going to live here you'll have to learn to deal with our money,' he said severely, tucking the groceries under one arm and opening the shop door for her. 'Farmers' wives need to be thrifty. And you'll have to shop more selectively as well,' he added reprovingly as she walked past him on unsteady legs.

'Carl——'

'You're probably quite good with money, which is a relief. Farmers don't live in luxury. But I'll take on photographic work when we need it, and you'll travel with me. I'll teach you to be my assistant——'

'Carl, will you listen to me!' She was almost dancing round him with rage.

He stopped, leaned back against the wall, and looked down at her, eyebrows raised. 'Well?'

'Of course I'm not going to marry you on Friday—or any other day!'

'I didn't give you a choice. Friday it is. And why not?'

'Well——' her voice faltered. A quirk of amusement was pulling at one corner of his mouth. 'For one thing, I don't love you!'

'Look into my eyes and say that,' he dared her, and she flushed and stared at his brown throat. 'You love me, little sister, and we both know it— now.'

'But you love Rachel!'

He began to walk again, and she had to run a few steps now and then to keep up with him. 'Now that's where we all kept going wrong. When Rachel went off to Paris I realised that I'd only been infatuated with her. If it had been love I'd have gone after her. No—Mike loves Rachel, Rachel loves Mike, you love me, and——' he stopped again, turned to look down at her, '—and I've loved you all my life. But I didn't realise it until you tripped over the paint-pot at the harbour and threw yourself at me.'

'I did not——'

'Shut up,' he ordered, and stopped her lips with his own. His kiss flared through her body, and she had to catch at his waist to keep herself upright. When he straightened she was quite unaware of the amused glances from passers-by, the giggles of a group of children who had paused to stare.

'I didn't even admit it to myself until I kissed you on the beach,' Carl went on, his voice suddenly husky. 'But you got me so angry that I decided to go ahead and marry Rachel and be the sort of brother-in-law you'd hate. Besides, I thought it was the only way to be near you.'

He frowned down at her. 'Haven't we all behaved like fools? Oh, my darling, thank heavens that we all came to our senses before it was too late! Come on, we've got a lot to do.'

Lisa ran after him as she strode across the harbour. 'Carl, we can't just decide things like that!' she protested, though the warmth of his kiss was still with her, telling her that this time nothing was going to tear Carl away from her again. 'I have to make plans, and arrangements——' she went on feebly as he put his free arm about her and half lifted her from the steps to the glass-bottomed boat.

He stowed the groceries in the cabin, started the engine, untied the mooring rope.

'I never thought nagging could sound so sweet! A lifetime of it isn't going to be enough,' he told her as he tossed his shirt down on the bench and took the wheel. 'In fact, I wish I'd had the sense to use you as the bride for my first wedding, instead of cancelling it. We'd have saved ourselves a lot of misery.'

'But where are we going?' She looked back at the harbour as the boat backed out, turned, and made for the open sea. The shed, the restaurant, the houses and people were beginning to recede as the engine picked up speed. A strip of water appeared between Lisa and the shore, and rapidly widened.

Carl reached for her and pulled her into the circle of his arms as he stood at the wheel. His chest was warm and hard beneath her cheek and she could feel the steady strong throb of his heart.

'We're going back to that little bay. We're going to swim ashore——'

'But my suit's back at the flat!'

He looked down at her, and his eyes sent a tingle over her body.

'You don't need a suit. There won't be anybody there to see you—except me. And when we reach the beach I'm going to take you in my arms and kiss you—and this time you won't turn to ice. Then——' His dark eyes were tender, loving, with a passion that, at last, was hers to take and to keep. 'Then,' said Carl huskily, '—then, my darling, my Melissa, you can talk to me of love.'